The Girl On The Wall

John Moore

Published in 2014 by FeedARead.com Publishing

A CIP catalogue record for this title is available from the British Library.

In memory of Bill Moore

CHAPTER 1

I laughed at the state of my boots, heavy and unwieldy with mud, as I trudged over a ploughed field in Gloucestershire.

"Bloody hell, Polly," I said, "what a fine mess I'm in. It's all your doing."

It all began in the pub, when she said, "Did you hear about that ban-the-bomb woman who has been told by someone in the know that there are underground shelters for the Government Ministers who'll run what's left of us, if we're hit with atom bombs?"

"What a ghastly thought. It's only eleven years since Hiroshima and Nagasaki. Have they faded from the memories of our rulers?"

"Not entirely. That's why they are making preparations. The country will be divided into regions, each with a commandant having unlimited power of Government."

I said, "It's like 1984, with the proles and Big Brother. There'll be meetings of selected privy councillors, field marshals, permanent secretaries…"

…."and one or two industrialists and newspaper proprietors," added Tony.

We laughed at that, and Polly said, "It's time for a protest movement against the atom bomb. There's a feeling building up but it hasn't got an organisational outlet yet. I've heard that a few people may be going down to look for one of the underground shelters next week-end and I thought of joining them. You can both come along, if you like. It's October half-term next week. It won't matter if you lose some sleep or don't get back till Monday morning."

Tony and I agreed very readily. "It's amazing," I said. "It's only 1956, but a nuclear war between the former allies seems a growing possibility. We would be a target, because we have American bases. No wonder a swell of opinion is forming in favour of getting rid of atom bombs."

"The details of where to meet will be told to me when I phone a friend. I'll tell you on Friday, but remember, it's top secret."

I nodded to her. I liked Polly's handsome features, soft, flowing hair and those luminous eyes that were sensitive to every shift of feeling in our conversation. She was sincere and idealistic, and would probably be very loving.

I picked up Polly and then Tony on Saturday morning and following her instructions drove into the Cotswolds, where I parked the car on the outskirts of Bourton. I led the way across springy and wet turf, fringed by trees only half dressed in leaves, towards Lower Slaughter, where a clear stream flowed briskly through the village.

Tony was impressed: "This place is really photogenic. You expect to see camera crews and Hollywood stars using it as a backcloth for romantic films."

"With nuclear bases not far away in Berkshire," Polly retorted. "That's right," I said. "This stream has a real function. It's more than just a pretty setting. The ducks will show the first signs of radio-active fall-out. We must come here regularly, to inspect their health. They'll be like the canaries that used to detect gas in the mines."

"Ha, ha," she said, "very far-fetched. There'll be no time for that. It'll be sudden annihilation."

We continued talking like friends on a normal day's outing, as we advanced through Upper Slaughter and turned in the direction of Naunton.

"Where exactly are we heading for?" I asked, as Polly studied her Ordnance Survey map. If we walk much further, it'll seem a long way back"

"I don't know too precisely, but it won't matter when we meet up with the others. It's a good walk and it'll do you good. I've got the map references. I'm told there's a mound looking a bit like an iron-age burial ground. We have to explore around there. There's a chain of underground rooms used in the war by military planners. They're officially closed down now but Jenny Hill, a woman I met on the Black Sash march in London, said they had been reopened. Our source of information is a mole in the Ministry of Defence."

"Very appropriate," said Tony. "That's how Churchill got the facts about German rearmament, twenty years ago. I've brought my Kodak. Perhaps a few pictures will interest people."

I hardly heard him, as Polly's mention of a woman's name spun in my head. The face of someone I once knew lit up in my memory. I turned towards her, asking myself if I should say anything, although I already knew the answer. "You say you met someone called Jenny?"

She saw through my casual manner and said with a smile, "Yes, is she a friend of yours? I know her well. A stocky, fair-haired woman with a nice smile. She's a nurse and was one of the founders of the Black Sash women's group. She has a doctor in tow. Or perhaps I should be careful what I tell you, in case you don't like what I say."

"We met once, some time ago, but it's long over."

"But the memory lingers on. She rang me up the other night, saying how much she would like to have come, if she hadn't been on duty at the hospital."

I wished she had been with us, but the embarrassment would have been great. Polly said, "Joe, you were married to Julie until last summer. You must have known Jenny quite a while ago."

"I was nearly twenty at the time." I paused. Polly had told me something about her life. I should do the same for her, but I wouldn't talk about Jenny. It was private, although we talked together frequently. I was chairman of the lecturers' union at West Midlands Central College, Polly was treasurer and Tony assistant secretary.

As we continued to climb, I looked at one of the lesser Cotswold landscapes.

"Lovely smooth curves! Fresh arable sloping down to the trees! And look at that mist waiting to be wiped away by the sun! This is great!" I shouted.

"Listen to him," said Polly. "He's like a kid from the city who's been taken into the country for the first time."

"It'll be even better after we've had a cup of tea," said Tony, the practical rambler, who was taking a thermos flask from his backpack, together with three bakelite cups. We lounged against a grey stone wall, which I also loudly admired.

Not long after that, we started a steep descent into a thick belt of trees.

"We're surely in the wilds now, and it's getting quite warm," Polly said, loosening her thick brown jacket.

"Your long skirt's a bit much for hiking," Tony said, putting a hand on Polly's arm. I glanced at them and saw them exchange smiles, devoid of embarrassment. They were just good friends.

There was a dramatic change of scene. We were near the foot of the hill when we glimpsed grey, ghostlike shapes of houses, and after five more minutes the curtain of trees was drawn back to reveal a large village.

"This is obviously Naunton," Polly told them. "It was so invisible; I thought it was still some way off."

I said excitedly, "Perhaps a secret base will come to light just as unexpectedly. We must have the gift of serendipity – or one of us, at least, and I don't' think it's me."

"Well, I don't really know what this gift is, but it sounds something good, so let's say Polly has it," Tony said cheerfully. Who's for a pint? The pub must just about be open."

But the pub didn't open until twelve, and there were forty minutes to go. Instead of being refreshed by beer and bacon sandwiches, we trudged on along a track leading from the village through a field of planted saplings and rising to a ridge. Tony ran up it and shouted back, "There's a new panorama of glowing hills and open sky, as Joe would say!"

"It can't be far away now," said Polly. "It's four miles beyond the river Windrush. We should see a crowd of people soon."

But it took us the best part of an hour to reach the right point according to the map, and I didn't think the grassy mound in the distance was anything out of the ordinary. I couldn't hear the noise of trumpets or motor bikes, and there was no crowd of placard -waving young protestors.

"Perhaps this isn't the place, I said. I wish now we'd brought the car at least as far as Naunton."

Polly suddenly confessed, "I was told by my friend Caroline that it was ninety per cent sure to be on today. She hoped to be able to ring me if the situation changed. Each one of the organisers telephones six people and they do the same and in no time you have a group of a hundred or more others alerted, with not much chance of the police getting to know of the demo in advance. But they need to feel confident that there's been no breach of security before they give the final signal."

"So we're probably on our own," I said angrily. "Why didn't she confirm with you? And why didn't you tell us the real situation?"

"I don't know. Perhaps she wasn't in when they tried to call her, or I missed her call. When we met this morning, it seemed a shame to waste an opportunity to have a good look round. I thought some other people would be here. But it was rather presumptuous of me. I'm sorry."

"So you should be," I said in a milder tone. You talk about equality of the sexes and then treat us like idiots incapable of deciding for ourselves whether we should risk a fruitless journey."

Her cheeks blushed. "I never really doubted there'd be a crowd."

Tony said, "Perhaps we should enjoy the day and go home, waiting for more reliable information in the future. A hundred people can trespass more safely than three."

Polly brushed away his hesitant words. "I know things haven't gone as I expected. But after coming all this way, we might as well do a reconnaissance."

"So long as we watch our steps, in more senses than one" I said. I had no real grudge against Polly, since I was enjoying the hunt, even if we found no fox.

As we started to pick our way down a stony slope, I guessed that Tony would stay with us, not wanting to lose face with Polly. Having got to the foot of the slope, I led the advance for a few hundred yards over rough grass and grey rock flecked with yellow to a hedge, expecting to see more of the same on the other side of it.

Instead, there was a notice warning, *Danger Keep Out. All Trespassers Will Be Prosecuted*, and then the ground fell away, and we were on the edge of an enormous quarry, cut partly out of yellow stone and partly clay, with a hill behind it. An area with a smooth surface in front of the quarry wall faced me, not far off two hundred feet below where I crouched. In the distance on our left a large pool

11

shimmered, behind piles of aggregates in weird shapes.

"Just look at this," I whispered, as though I could be overheard, Cotswold limestone must have been cut here centuries ago. It doesn't look as though it's a quarrying business today. Unless it's an abandoned site, it's likely to be or some kind of government operation. We may have hit the bull's-eye."

"Well, if we're going on, we'd better find a way down." Polly sounded determined, and so was Tony when he said he had come far enough. "I'm sorry, but I don't like it. We came here under the impression that we were joining up with a crowd, who would attract the newspapers and so create publicity about preparations for a nuclear war. I can see trespass leading to arrest and possible imprisonment and the loss of our jobs."

"That's a very extreme view, Tony," she said sharply."

"Sorry. I'm returning to Bourton, where I'll wait for you. If you get back late and I'm not by the car, I'll have found a bus to take me back. Is that all right? At least, I'm a witness to your whereabouts, if things should go seriously wrong."

"They won't," said Polly, still impatient with him, though she added in a conciliatory tone, "but if they did, it would be useful to have you at liberty."

I guessed Polly and I walked nearly a hundred yards round the lip of the quarry before coming to a less precipitous drop, with yellow stone pieces giving footholds for a descent. I soon made a tear in the leg of my flannels and paused in a gully to wait for Polly, who had taken off her top jacket and tied it round her waist, above which her blouse rode high.

"What are you staring at? You know you've seen the female body before."

"Yes, all right." I put a hand gently on her shoulder, but she removed it. Her face went red and she averted her eyes from me for a full minute. She seemed to come to a decision and said tremulously, "There's something I have until now only told to Tony. I see another woman – we've been close, on and off, since we were at university. We have men friends, but we don't go to bed with them."

I was stunned by her disclosure. "You mean you have sex together?"

"Of course – we're human, and we also have a close friendship."

Homosexuality was not a live issue, as no-one understood it or talked about it. The idea of Polly being labelled grossly indecent was preposterous. I had long ago thought Oscar Wilde's conviction was monstrous. I thanked her for being so frank and for trusting me. "We will stay good friends, starting with our visit to the underworld."

"That stands with me, too. I'm being a bit too solemn. I like you, as well as Tony, though I understand him better. He's less of a romancer than you, with your talk of canaries and fall-out."

"Okay, governess. Let's press on."

I was still startled by Polly's revelation, but the task at hand took away the feeling. I thought I might have falls or scrapes on the way down but we were soon sitting at the bottom of the cliff. I relaxed and said, "Isn't this the point at which a steel-grey

Landrover drives up and three men in black tracksuits and balaclavas stand, facing us grimly, with bulges in their trousers that don't mean they're pleased to see us?"

"Stop that! It makes me scared. This place is probably deserted, so that we'll see only a rusty bike and some old tyres. Let's walk on."

This time, after brushing the yellow dust off my windcheater, I found our roles reversed and trailed after her in a straight walk to the smooth surface. Suddenly, she stopped and said, "Look at this."

She was peering at some earth-brown double doors, discernible through a gap in the trees. They gave me an impression of formidable strength, as I ran up to them. They were made of steel and when I hit them there was no sound, as though they were feet thick.

"I think this place, whatever it is, would resist a whole gang of burglars using crowbars or firearms. Of course, it could be just a store for army boots, rifles, baking tins, Bofor guns and hundreds of tons of other supplies."

But she seemed shaken by the sight of the doors. "I must admit, my bravado is ebbing away. "This is something really worrying."

"Not really, or not yet. If we let our imaginations run riot, anything could be behind the brown doors, perhaps a community of zombies reviving corpses, or a coven of Dr Mengele's medical heirs carrying out experiments on convicts. But that's plain daft. Let's carry on round the quarry. We could rest up in the bushes at the far side and work out what to do.

What I can't fathom is why we haven't seen motor tracks and any obvious way out for vehicles."

"There must be another door at road level on the other side of the cavern or chamber on the other side of these doors."

"Maybe," I countered, "but when we scanned the mound from the lane, it seemed surrounded by fields and hedges."

"We don't know how extensive the area inside is."

"Well, I suppose it could be miles long," I said dismissively, "but we must be practical. It's hardly likely to be the eighth wonder of the world."

"I suppose there could be another quarry hollowed out inside the doors. It could be a gigantic receptacle for the bodies of victims of a nuclear strike."

"That's just morbid talk. It presupposes that there would be transport to carry them here from the cities that would be reduced to rubble. Come on, let's move."

I led the way to the sparse bushes about forty yards away, and we slumped down on mangy grass. Polly told me to curb my imagination and not to go on about zombies, as it disturbed her. We sat saying nothing and as it was a warm Autumn I stretched out with my head on my arm. Before I nodded off I heard a gentle snore from Polly. When I awoke, I saw from my watch I had slept for twenty minutes. I looked at the doors and saw that they were open, and several men in blue overalls were standing on the threshold, looking up at a descending helicopter.

"Of course," I thought. "The quarry floor is a landing pad." Then I put a hand over Polly's mouth while I woke her as I stared at the drama. The aircraft was dappled in grey and green patches, suggestive of military camouflage. It was long enough to occupy a good half of the landing pad, which I estimated was about thirty yards square. The engine roar that bounced back off the quarry walls died away and its blades became listless and then stopped turning. The crew of two men alighted and the figures in blue overalls clambered inside and began to unload packing cases and what seemed to be office equipment, including desks.

"We can't give up now," I whispered. "I'd like to get inside and have a look round. Why the hell didn't I think to ask Tony for the loan of his camera? He didn't even take a picture of the quarry."

"It's very scary," she said, and I don't think we should try to go on any further. It will take a long time for these guys to finish their work. At the moment, I think Tony was right, but I'm not yellow. I'm up for it up for it, if you want to try again."

"Okay. You can't go back to Bourton on your own, and anyway the light's already starting to fade. We wouldn't see much even if they left the gates unlocked."

We scrambled back to the top of the quarry and lay panting in the grass. Polly had slipped on the rock and bruised her leg. Her face was stained with grime and tears.

"Sorry, Joe," she said. "I was feeling shattered after all that walking and couldn't face the unknown. I'll come out again next Saturday if you like."

"Make it a fortnight's time. It's the Michaelmas dance next week and I arranged to go with Trevor and his wife."

"I'm off to see my family in Bristol on Saturday week."

"And the next Saturday I'm taking mother to a concert in the Town Hall. Then we're almost in December and we'll be in the grip of Christmas shopping mania. Nobody will want to come with us, even if it's not snowing. We'll keep it flexible, but we'll be back with reinforcements, I hope. One thing is sure. This base is not going to go away."

She agreed and I helped her limp back to Naunton, where the pub having opened for two hours was closed again. It opened at six o'clock and as it was after five I was tempted to hang on for a pint, but it was a selfish thought and so we both leaned on the wall outside with a few people waiting for a bus home.

"It's the Bourton bus!" Polly shrieked. She kissed me on the cheek and I patted her on the shoulder. I found that the day in her company and the revelation of her sexual feelings had drained off most of my amorous interest in her, leaving behind a friendship that I felt sure was real. I was disappointed by our failure to enter the doors in the rock, but not too upset. They would still be there, whenever we were. If we were on the edge of discovery of a big hideaway for some people who were considered worth saving from the atom bomb, it could be politically explosive. It had to be pursued. I felt like the ramblers who climbed Kinder

Scout in Derbyshire in defiance of the KEEP OUT notices. This time the stakes were higher.

Tony was nowhere to be seen in Bourton and we concluded he was somewhere on a tortuous bus route. My 1936 Morris 8 then set off for home at a steady pace. Polly was restored to her usual lively self, and we talked generally. I mentioned that my car's windscreen had been smashed two nights ago, though I took some of the blame myself for leaving the car out on the road all night. "The police stated the obvious – it seems like someone has a grudge against me. They say their man will keep an eye on my place when he passes, but there's not much they can do unless I can give them a name."

"I've good reason to be concerned about street hooliganism. My parents came to Britain from Poland as Jewish refugees and joined the demonstrations against Moseley, in the 'thirties."

"You're right. If it can be labelled "fascist," it's always got to be opposed, even when the mass discontent on which it thrives does not exist. I think my trouble is more likely to be an act of spite by people smarting over the loss of Suez. They think of it as national humiliation or some such indignity."

I saw Polly's cheeks aflame, as she spoke vehemently. "I support the Egyptians and feel ashamed of Israel. But as far as its right to exist is concerned, I'm all for it. There's no argument. There's still room for a separate Palestinian state."

"I'm with you there, all the way".

Polly changed the subject. "Joe, I'm not going to talk about the woman I referred to on the walk. Let me say a little about my family background. My parents were socialists and if that wasn't bad enough in Warsaw in the 'twenties, they also fell foul of the strong anti-Semitism. My father was forced out of his profession as a dentist, but they were lucky enough to have enough savings to get to Britain, where I was born. What's your story?"

After the day's exertions, I wanted a quiet ride, with occasional exchanges of remarks, but her sympathetic tone made her enquiry hard to resist. I thought for a minute before saying, "It's the colourful details that stay in my mind. I could be woken at night by voices or coughing and when I crept downstairs I would find the living room full of people, mainly men. Tough-looking old fellows would say things like, 'Hallo Joe, aren't you a big boy! How old are you now - seven?'

"Dorothy, my mother, told me that she did not like it when they didn't go home, even after she had made cups of tea. They talked till midnight and dropped ash on the linoleum. They were in the Party and most of them had no jobs to go to in the morning. There was a tram driver with a rumbling cough, whose words came in a rush as he chopped the air with one hand. 'It's 1936 and no better, seven years after the start of the capitalist slump. I dare anyone to say things are not better in the Soviet Union. They're making great strides, and there's no unemployment.'

"A stocky, red-faced man had a big bulge on his right temple and I once asked my father, 'Is Lumpy coming tonight?' I was told not to make fun of the man's swelling, as he was injured in the Great War. Another man, known as Old Hairy because of the hair growing out of his ears, used to say to me, 'How are the hyenas today?' I never knew how to answer him, but I was spared embarrassment, since at that point my mother would send me up to my room, her parting words on one occasion being, 'You've had your moment in the limelight, Joe. Now it's back to bed."

It was unusual for Polly not to get many words in edgeways but all she said was, "I can see them, Joe, victims of the depression."

By tacit agreement, we sat quietly for the rest of the ride home until I dropped my friend off in her road and drove home. I stopped to buy fish and chips, which I ate rapaciously before going to bed, where I lay awake, thinking about the memories she had stirred up.

I saw my father, Edward, tall, with brown, wavy hair, smiles and laughter. When I was quite young, he told me stories at bedtime and held me in his arms when someone on the wireless sang, *Little Man, you've had a busy day*.

Once, when I was about three, mother took me on "visiting day" to see Edward, who was inside a little shed, which was half-open at the front, so that he looked a bit like the woman who sold tickets at the picture house. 'He shouldn't be here, Joe,' she said. "He was put in prison, after a meeting of the unemployed at the town hall. A policeman told the lie that Edward had punched someone."

I knew my lovely dad would never do that. "Why did they do that to him?"

"Because they wanted him out of the way, as he was the leader of the unemployed workers."

"Can't he get a job?"

"No. He has done his best but the jobs aren't there to be had in the slump. Anyway, he's blacklisted."

On the great day of Edward's release, I kicked a ball around with him all evening until it was dark, trying to make up for lost time. One afternoon, later in the year, I held my father's fingers to my cheek, as we walked round the frozen pool near where we lived, in Birmingham.

I pleaded with him to come and walk on the ice with me. Edwards lifted a boot and showed the sole worn down to the sock. "I'll mend it tonight," he said, and I hadn't the heart to remind him there would probably be a meeting.

Once or twice I sat on the handcart which they pushed round the streets of our council estate, collecting tins of beans and condensed milk for the Republicans in the Spanish Civil War, laughing, waving a red flag and singing snatches of *The Red Airman's Song: Fly higher and higher and higher…*.

I wondered why the Russians were sometimes called Soviets or the Soviet Union. I knew I had been named after their leader, Joe Stalin, whose plaque in white plaster stood on the mantelpiece in the front room.

"The Russians are sending help to Spain" said Dorothy. "They help the people."

'Like Robin Hood or Jesus?'

"In a way, yes, but they don't believe in God."

A young man in the next road on the council estate died after drinking a bottle of disinfectant. On the day of the funeral, Dorothy said he had been fed up with not having work and being poor, and that it would not have happened if he had lived in Russia. The black clothes and the dray horses disturbed me, but when I asked about dying, she replied casually, "The man has died and they are putting him into the earth in an orange box. That's the finish for him. There's no pie in the sky, only clouds."

The vivid picture of orange boxes in the ground flashed into my mind whenever I passed a greengrocer's. I saw half-inch gaps between the wooden slats of the boxes lying on the pavement and wondered if they were covered over or if the bodies could be seen through them.

There was a catchy tune sung by boys in the street, with words I did not understand. *Will you come to Abyssinia, will you come? Bring your own ammunition and your gun. Mussolini will be there, shooting millions in the air...*

Mother said it was a disgusting song, typical of Fascists, who hated black people.

My favourite time was going out on my own by tram to fish in the pool, clutching the long cane with the small net on the end. Most of the flotilla of minnows would snake away but I usually went home blissful, with a few captives in my jam jar. I wondered how it could be better in Russia.

I was nearly ten when one night in bed, my mouth went dry and I felt the beat of my heart when I heard Dorothy sobbing downstairs. It was not like my mother, who was quiet and always talked to me calmly. Tip-toeing to the landing, I heard some of her words:

'You don't say you love me. You are away so often, I wonder if you care for me anymore."

My father's voice faltered, as he answered her: 'I'm doing it for Joe. Unless the people wake up there will be war, and who knows what will happen to us? In the Soviet Union I should have to go to even more meetings'

"I was tense with anxiety until I heard them laughing together again, buoyed up by the thought of Russia.

"The next day was Sunday September 3 1939, when I went on my usual bus ride to have Sunday dinner with Grandma. I hoped I would see my Aunt Mary, who brought me little bags of misshapen chocolates rejected by Cadbury's, where she was a supervisor. Sometimes she took me to the pictures.

"The aroma of veal and stuffing, which I can still smell over the years, was in the yard, as I touched the wooden rollers of the iron-framed mangle that stood five feet high against the wall. One of my uncles had jokingly called it Stalin but it seemed a funny thing to say, as Stalin was a good man. Then I heard a cry from over the wall. 'It's Chamberlain on the wireless,' roared the man next door. 'We're at war!'

Grandma ran into the yard and tears trickled down her cheeks. "September 3 1939," she said angrily. "Not twenty years since the Armistice after the last war!"

Throughout the afternoon, uncles and aunts came on buses and trams back to the old house like homing pigeons. My parents came in, holding hands. They put their arms round me and stroked my cheeks.

They were all much quieter than usual as they passed the bread and butter from one to another at the polished round table, while Grandma, usually a merry talker, just chattered to herself about gas masks and blackout curtains.

Aunt Mary's mood became combative, after she lit a cigarette. She was as tall as her brothers and just as assertive. "What about Russia?" she said. "When are they coming in with us? Or are they sticking with their new friend, Hitler?"

My father answered coolly, "You wait and see. The Russians will fight the Fascists - just as they did in Spain."

Mary shrugged her shoulders. A haze of cigarette smoke spread through the room. Grandma seemed to fear the gloaming and lit the lamp at the faintest fading of the light. When she pulled the strings to make the tiny flame ignite inside the mantle, I said, "You are like the lady who switches on the Christmas lights in the town."

Grandma's laughter did not divert the conversation. Uncle Frank said, "This is Chamberlain's doing, of course. He handed Czechoslovakia to Hitler, whereas he could have made an alliance with Russia and stopped him in his tracks."

Aunt Mary turned to him in anger: "That's clap-trap. You ought to live in Russia. I'm British and proud of it."

My father said, "Who says Chamberlain's going to fight the Fascists? He might be making diplomatic moves behind the scenes even now to fight against the Soviet Union."

Mary came back with spirit. "I say again, What about the Nazi-Soviet Pact?"

Edward replied with equal force, "The problem has been, as Frank said, Western inaction on collective security. Munich came before the Pact. Russia saw the danger of being manoeuvred into fighting Germany on its own and acted to prevent it."

Uncle Frank and Uncle Bill gave murmurs of approval. Mary's cheeks reddened and she stormed at them, "Russia! You go on about it all the time! It's no paradise. The people go around with cloth on their feet instead of shoes."

I could hardly believe that he heard her right. I cried out, "But they have jobs to go to in the morning."

They all clapped and cheered me, even my aunt, who said, "I know what you mean, Joey, but I'd rather be unemployed here than have a job in Russia."

A roar of protest rose from the brothers. "You've never been unemployed!" one of them shouted.

"But Grandma was well used to their rows. Picking up a broom handle from behind the door, she cried out, "That'll do! We have too much to think about today. Stop it or get out into the garden, all of you."

It was enough to break the tension, but I was upset. It was partly because was aunt was stroking my hair as if I were a baby, instead of a boy of nine.

But the main reason was that she had criticised Russia. It made me feel very slightly unsure, like a stranger in the land of my parents' dreams.

During the next few months of half-time schooling at the beginning of the war, I didn't think much about politics. When we went to school, we had our gas masks swinging on our shoulders, with little cases labelled, *Carry me with you wherever you go.* I spent the afternoons with friends, walking on the shoulder-high walls of some new houses on which work had been stopped. Once, after creeping through a cornfield, we came to an orchard where the apples were larger and sweeter than they had ever known. We were tipsy with excitement and the feeling of brotherhood. I strutted in front, leading the singing *of South of the Border*. Paradise was here and now.

Mother said she I hoped the day would come when she could throw the damn ration books into the Bourneville pool. But at least there was some money to spend now that there were all the jobs in the war factories.

"I no longer held dad's hand or sat on mother's lap or thought much about Russia until the Germans invaded it. Then everything changed. Russia became the new heroic ally, and my father led the trade union campaign in his factory to increase production. He was even decorated for his work, and the local paper had a headline about his investiture at Buckingham Palace. It sounds bizarre. I wish I had been there with Tony's Kodak to record the monarch and the republican making common cause.

I started at the grammar school and in the oak-panelled hall the pianist played the Jupiter melody from the *Planet Suite.* As the school sang the accompanying words, *And there's another country, I've heard of long ago, Most dear to those who love her, Most great to those that know,* I was startled. It was just as they had described Russia. Even the Headmaster standing on the dais in his black gown seemed to think it was better over there. I knew he did not really believe that but all the same I imagined the dais draped in the red flag and alongside it Edward, Dorothy, Lumpy, Hairy and the rest of the comrades, with the tram driver coughing and punching at the air."

CHAPTER 2

Work in the upper school took up more and more time and I lost touch with my parents' old comrades, though I knew that Lumpy cut a figure as a forceful sergeant in the Home Guard. I was more concerned by how few girls I met. In town on VE night, I encountered a group of women in their twenties and one of them gave me a passionate kiss, before they moved on.

Granddad Butler had done his best to help me after Edward died. He took me to football matches, the pictures and the Hippodrome, where nude young women stood on stage in careful, statuesque poses. I shan't forget a trip to Weston super Mare in 1945, when I was sixteen. It was supposed to be an exercise in befriending girls, in accordance with his stated philosophy that girls were like pebbles on the beach; lose one and there were always plenty waiting to be picked up.

His vanity had led Granddad into folly in his middle years, when he moved in with a pub landlady much younger than he was. After a year or two, the landlady got rid of him and he had to move into lodgings. Grandma, ever the merry talker, had kept the family together and did not miss her husband, who was only allowed into the house on Christmas night. He would sit quietly, sipping his stout, until his turn for a song came round. Then he would sing deeply and sadly,

When the poppies bloom again, I'll remember you

On the coach I watched him eyeing two young women sitting across the aisle from us. When the coach stopped at the seafront, Granddad followed the girls across the promenade, down some steps to the beach, where we sat a few feet behind them.

He became tense and watched intently as the girls undid their blouses, only to reveal the tops of their swimming costumes. They politely declined Granddad's offer to rub cream on their shoulders. One of them said, "We'll be going into the water before long. How about you, old man? I suppose you can swim, can't you?"

To my horror he started to take his clothes off. Amazingly, he was wearing clos-fitting trunks and after a lordly wave he drew in his belly, trotted to the water's edge and plunged into the sea. He shot of with the power and grace of a dolphin. "He must have been a champion swimmer, the girl cried . He must be seventy, if he's a day – randy old goat!"

Then someone called out that he was nearly back. His crawl was propelling him much more slowly to the beach, until he stopped in the shallows, like a motor boat without fuel. He drifted to the water's edge and collapsed like a beached whale.   At my touch he said, "I didn't think I was going to make it back."

His head fell back and one girl started to press on his chest to expel the water.   The cry went up,

"Quick, get an ambulance! They'll telephone from the pub."

Suddenly, the onlookers gave a shout of surprise, quickly turning to derision, as Granddad turned on his side, flung his arms round the neck of one of the girls and gave her a warm kiss on the lips.

"Don't send for the ambulance," he said in a sprightly manner. I feel much better now."

"You are an old fox, as well as a goat," she shouted, and stormed off the beach with her friend, leaving me with red cheeks.

"What a bloody fool," I said and felt inclined to follow them. Then I partly regretted my disloyalty, but did not forget my lesson in how not to befriend girls. It was my last excursion with Granddad.

School was to be succeeded by university, but first came National Service. Almost at the end of my time in the RAF a momentous meeting took place.

The train back to camp was ready to depart. A light breeze blew the smoke onto the platform. I had taken a seat and was alone in the compartment, looking out of the window at the evening sun touching the brown of the bench seats but missing the underside of the wrought iron canopy over the platform.

As the train hissed loud and stamped out of the station, the compartment door slid open and a girl entered. She sat down on the opposite bench and said, "I hope you don't mind."

I stuttered, "Not at all," and to cover my confusion took out a packet of Players and thrust it towards her."

"No thanks. I don't smoke."

"Nearly everyone does in the Forces. You wouldn't be a regular in one of the Services, would you?

"No, I'm a first year nurse in Shrewsbury. It's not very different from the A.T.S."

"I'm stationed at Bridgnorth. It's easy for the permanent staff. What's the discipline like for you?"

"We stand to attention when the consultants come round. Or we hide in the sluice."

I put the cigarettes back in my pocket and looked at her from the corner of my eyes. She was stocky, but slim in the waist, with fair, short hair clinging to her head. I liked the smile starting in her eyes and spreading across her face.

I looked away but it seemed she had read me and liked my interest. Her friendliness relaxed me. I wanted to run the tips of my fingers over her brow and cheek and then kiss her lips for a full minute while she closed her eyes like a film star.

After a few minutes silence, in the hope that the girl would not detect a slight physical stirring, I leaned over slightly to make the thick trousers more tent-like and protective. Her eyes again lit up, as she pointed to a folded pamphlet sticking out of the pocket of my greatcoat on the seat. The title was obscured, apart from the word Socialism that stuck out defiantly.

"Not exactly No Orchids for Miss Blandish, or even an Agatha Christie," I said. "A pamphlet like that one got me into trouble."

"How come?"

"A young officer ordered me not to bring it into the unit. I went through the grievance procedure and won. So now I read it where they can see me and it's become very boring."

I seemed to have fanned her interest. "That took some doing," she said, but flushed at her own words of praise. She leaned forward eagerly and said, "When I was twelve, I played around my mother while she put up exhibitions about Russia, in the foyer of the local cinema."

"Yes, I remember. There was terror and loss of life, but kids were often more excited than afraid. At school we used to compare fragments of bombs collected after air raids, and occasionally scraps of parachute harness from landmines."

"I was with my mother in Coventry when the big Blitz smashed up half the houses. Ours was saved but we had no water or electricity or gas and lots of people we knew were killed. We were afraid then."

She sank back on the upholstery, and said, "By the way, my name is Jenny. I know yours begins with a J, as well. I can see it on the side of your kitbag. Nurses have to be literate these days."

"I don't doubt it.   I'm Joe. Did you go straight from school into nursing, as I did to the Forces?"

"No. I worked in one or two sales jobs, but didn't fit in. I didn't think the customer was always right."

"Tell me more."

"One time, I was a receptionist at a department store. A young man came in and said, 'Aren't you a new girl? I come here now and again to talk business with your boss. He knows me well.'

"When I said I'd rather not accept his invitation to dinner, he became very insistent with his hands, until I slapped him hard. I was sacked on the spot. But I expect you were reading Latin then."

"You did the right thing. Don't talk yourself down. I don't know much Latin, and the only wage I earned before I was called up was in holiday jobs."

As her cheeks flushed, I smiled, and said, "I'm a corporal because I'm in Education, teaching English and Maths. I also lead discussions on Current Affairs, much to the annoyance of some of the officers, who are mostly Tories. One of them thinks Churchill lost in 1945 because of ballot rigging. But it's an easy life and I've met some unusual people."

"Such as?"

"Like the topless cooks heavily coated in lipstick and rouge, slapping bubble and squeak on our plates."

"Surely, the cooks wear bras."

"No, they're men."

"She   laughed uproariously, as I played to the gallery:

"Then there's Sergeant Bert Brummit, who did a real job in the war, but now is in a sort of alcoholic semi-retirement. He's an expert at mixing swears words with ordinary speech, so they seem no more shocking than commas and full stops. His friend, Corporal Blood, is also very good at that, but far behind old Bert."

"Don't tell me there is really someone called Corporal Blood."

"Oh yes, there is.   He's a quiet, obliging man

helping in the camp library. After work he becomes a drinking companion of Brummit in the pubs.

"Brummit once drank fourteen whiskies straight off for a dare, to my knowledge. I was taking my turn with a squad of men in the nearby town on policing duty, to pick up anyone from the camp who was making a public nuisance, which usually meant getting roaring drunk. There was a great noise coming from a pub and so we looked inside. There was Brummit with the whiskies lined up in front of him, and a crowd of airmen urging him on. He picked up one glass after another and swigged down the drinks. Then he sat down by his mate and resumed his conversation, with no obvious ill effects."

"That was crazy. At that rate, cirrhosis of the liver will get him, for sure. Tell me how he speaks. Don't worry, nurses know every swear word in the dictionary, as well as those that aren't."

"I think we should have to be better friends, before I could bring myself to talk to you like he does."

"Pity - I'm curious. Perhaps I'll ask you about him again, some day."

"I hope so."

We both looked away, aware of what we had said, and I wondered if she was as surprised as I was at how well we were hitting it off. I almost wished I were remaining at the camp, so as to be near to her. But I said, "I'm off to university in three weeks' time. That's more than father could ever say. Things have got better for us."

Her spirited reply surprised me: "Yes, but look at

those pictures above your head. They must have been in that frame for twenty-five years. Men in monocles alighting a Rolls Royce or pointing guns in the air, with gillies carrying dead birds at their heels."

"The women with diamonds and silver foxes look as though they are part of the catch!"

"It's still the same system. Nothing has really changed."

"No, the hyenas are still out there - that's just a phrase a man I knew was fond of using. It kept me awake at night, when I was a kid. By the way, do your parents think like you?"

"My mother used to, but she's given up now. She was pleased when I became a nurse. She said the NHS was the model of her ideal society."

"Giving to everyone according to their needs?"

"That's right."

"What about your dad?"

"I never knew him. One of my mother's friends stayed at her place after a meeting, and I was the result of a very brief affair. She hardly ever mentioned him to me, and I've never tried to find him, for fear of hurting her."

"It must have been hard going."

"It was. She believed that women should be independent and live with the results of their own actions. But she would have lost her job as a teacher if the authorities had known about me."

"I'm sorry. I've some idea of the difficult time she must have had. I was brought up by my mother, after we lost dad in the Italian campaign."

She leaned over and squeezed my hand. "I'm

sorry," she said.

"It was in 1943. I used to have a letter from him every week, until he was killed in action. I had a breakdown for a fortnight. I still see him coming over the threshold of our house."

"It must have been very hard on your mother."

"Yes, I owe everything to her. She put her arms round me when she broke the news, but her composure was short-lived and we cried together. She was already working part-time but found a full-time job to keep us both, while I stayed on at school.

"Granddad, on my father's side, also did his best for me. He was a conceited old man, who left Grandma for another woman who kept a pub. As a small boy I heard my uncles talk of her long, wavy hair and breasts like the peaks of Snowdonia.

"I can't imagine it lasting very long."

"You're right. He'd been a fairly prosperous coppersmith, but the slump of the 'thirties destroyed everything and the landlady got rid of him. Anyway, he took me to football matches, the pictures and the Hippodrome, to see the nude ladies standing on stage in careful poses."

"It must have been a thrill for you."

"It helped me overcome a few inhibitions."

"Not too many, I hope."

I eyed the supple movements of Jenny's body as she smiled at my spiel, and decided to try a party piece. I said solemnly, "Let's see what is written in your hand. I learned it from the gypsies, at the foot of the Carpathian mountains."

She showed me her palm and my cheek felt scorched, close to hers.

"It looks like you'll survive, despite the atom bomb. Yes, one day you will be a very old lady."

I spun the tale and thought perhaps my chance had come. I had visions of lighting the blue paper and awaiting the cascade of lights in her eyes. Perhaps the tip of my tongue could graze her lip...

She drew back slightly. Her words confirmed that she had read my thoughts.

"Seduction isn't like switching on the ignition. It takes time. You can't rush anyone into feeling what you'd like them to feel for you. Not even Granddad could do that."

My cheeks burned and I sat well back, wondering at the sexual confidence shown by men I had met in the Air Force. They were accustomed to casual sex, obtained easily with girls met in dance halls or pubs. At least, that was what they said. I used to wonder how tall their stories were, though I always nodded wisely as if from worldly or perhaps even similar personal experience. I said, "I'm sure I have a lot to learn. I might be looking for a tutor. Bridgnorth is not too far from Shrewsbury."

She leaned over and gave me a quick, soft touch on his lips with a finger, before saying, "I'm not really qualified myself. We should both need L - plates. Young men asking if they can take us out besiege the nurses' home. When we meet them at the hospital dances, it's all Dutch courage. Some of the girls will put up with these fellows even when they're horribly drunk, but I won't. I'd rather stay single and be a nurse for the rest of my life."

I thought about one or two tipsy scenes in which I had played a small role. "Drink gets you going in a

37

crowd. I get a bit merry, but not horribly so. Going straight from school into the Forces, you think two pints are very daring."

"I didn't have you in mind," she said earnestly. "I didn't mean to speak as though I was telling you off."

"I didn't take it that way."

We laughed, and I felt confident enough to ask her for a date, but then the train started to slow down and my eloquence deserted me. What if she politely declined my invitation or said it wasn't that simple?

The train lurched to a standstill. It was at the station – Wolverhampton already.

"Hell's bells!" she exclaimed, "is this it?"

She scribbled her hospital address on an envelope and thrust it into my hand. We exchanged impulsive, light kisses, and I rushed off to join the queue for the bus back to camp.

The next weekend I was on duty and the one after that I went home for mother's birthday. I wrote to Jenny a couple of times, a little shyly, aware that we had pretended to be closer than we could possibly be, in such a short time together. I told her about my degree course and how I wondered if I would feel at ease surrounded by public-school boys.

She sent back entertaining accounts of her nursing experiences but also said she realised I would soon be moving a long way off to a very different world in which I would make many new friends, so it might be best if they waited till I had come through the furnace. We could be completely different people by that time.

I knew she was leaving the door open for us to meet before I went away, if I took the initiative, but her argument about new friendships was obviously right, and the time weeks fled by.

I left the RAF just before term started, and went from camp to college, where there were quadrangles instead of parade grounds, and the sounds of public school accents rather than the gruff tones of Sergeant Brummit and Corporal Blood. I sat down to dinner in a great hall, in which silver cutlery, polished oak and coloured academic hoods shone in light reflected from the men of destiny and college patrons staring from the walls.

I didn't forget Jenny in the next three years, though my relationships with other girls were exciting distractions. None lasted very long; and looking back at them a few years on was like taking out of their box the lead soldiers which I had been given, one Christmas. There was the quiet, slender one, the historian with the soulful, innocent-looking eyes belying her sense of mischief, who let me stay overnight a few times when her landlady was away. I met a physicist at a dance but the affair seemed to me to resemble one of her laboratory exercises. It petered out because we never met outside her rooms.

There were one or two others with whom I went on the river, and that was that. They mostly had well-off professional families that had imbued them with a degree of self-confidence that I could not match, but they were all nice women, and looking back I knew I could have tried harder to build friendships. I was so self-centred and emotionally detached from all of them. I wished I could start again and make haste slowly.

People I knew quite well in my college all seemed destined for the City, the higher ranks of the civil service or business management. I knew that I could continue to express my political views openly, rather than have to change them for the sake of the material rewards expected by my college friends in careers where extreme views would be a big hindrance.

Then suddenly I was no longer caught up in the whirl of student life, but working at the Midlands Central College, near to where mother lived. That was the least I owed to her. I wasn't sure if I wanted to keep to her political course or even put down long-term roots in the Midlands. Mother would understand if eventually I sought new fields, perhaps in London. I needed time to plot my course. I sent Jenny a letter saying how I was getting on, and received a friendly reply, saying she was married. I wanted to telephone her, but a sense of the ridiculous made me laugh it off. I visualised her bottling fruit, driving the family Hillman, helping her children with their schoolwork, and making love to her husband, when the television set was put to sleep for the night. She wouldn't be working at the hospital now. She would rarely think of me. I had my chance once and she was willing, but I put my own short-term interests first. I could do nothing now.

However, by 1954 I had settled down well at the college, telling myself I could do without women, at least for the time being. I took out a mortgage on two living rooms, a kitchen and a bathroom on the first floor of a large Edwardian house surrounded by trees and lawns that I did not have to mow. It was blissful to sink into my second-hand leather armchair and listen to a record on the Dansette, which had to do until I could afford a radiogram. I decided that the sad, romantic but vibrant strains of Rachmaninov's Second Symphony summed up my feelings.

I would stare at my paintings on the walls. Two agreeable young ladies, one playing a mandolin, looked down from Matisse's *Magic*, as copied by an artist friend. "If I feel lonely, "I said, "I shall only have you two for company. Let me know though, if three's a crowd."

+

CHAPTER 3

]

A week after the first Cotswold enterprise, the Michaelmas Dance was warming up when I arrived. Dark suits and bright dresses were swirling, and the smell of smoke and beer was spreading through the Edwardian, panelled hall of the College. The bar was crowded with suited men; I listened in to their conversation and heard many condemnations of "Bloody Nasser" and his nationalisation of the Canal.

I walked up to them and called out, "Blame Eden, not the Egyptians. The Canal's in their country, not ours!"

Their main response was no more than cheerful thumbs-down or fingers-up gestures of disapproval, as my opposition to a Suez war was well-known in the College, where I had been a lecturer for four years. One man stepped forward with flushed face, shouting, "Shut it, you! We'll fight if we have to. Any more talk like that and you'll have it coming to you."

"Not from you, you fat blighter! What did you fight for last time, Malcolm – free speech?"

I had some support from an Accountancy lecturer, Ted Groves, who was in his late thirties and had been one of the airborne troops who landed at Arnhem. A quiet man, he raised his voice to Malcolm: "The first time you see a man bleeding in a ditch with a bullet in his chest, you will ask yourself if the Canal is worth it."

The incident faded, as our attention was diverted by the shapely figure of Kathleen from General Studies, who walked delicately by, stiletto heels clicking, saying casually, "Excuse me, Joe," as she brushed against my arm. She made a beeline to the College Principal and invited him to have the dance that was just starting.

As the girl with the four-piece band sang the sentimental words, *Memories are made of this,* I felt a stab of emotion, but said to myself, not for the first time, that the only way to shake off the debris of my broken marriage to Julie was to find someone new. The two-year relationship was not always on my mind but it quite often came back to me on a wave of emotion. I watched Kathleen bow to Mr Jones and his grey-haired wife, with no apparent concern for the cool manner of the other College people at their table. But she kept her body away from the Principal when they were on the floor and nodded deferentially to his remarks, as though she was merely a junior colleague.

Her flowing movements, flushed cheeks, and full bosom stirred me. I fancied a close encounter with her, stroking her face and neck with one hand, and holding her compressed waist with the other.

A voice behind me said, "She's a bold one. Or perhaps she's daft enough to think no one knows what's going on. You should bear her in mind though. She's only thirty and not daft, though not brilliant. I could see you wondering what she was like under her emerald dress."

43

The Union secretary Trevor had come over from the bar with two pints. He was with his wife, Margaret, who said, in a rising Welsh tone, "Don't be so cheeky. Joe can find his own women. Look at his nice features and wavy hair. He's very eligible. Mind you don't spill beer over his smart, navy-blue suit."

I glanced at her ample figure contrasting with Trevor's wiry physique. Her mobile rear was impressive as she walked, but I feared it would be ponderous in years to come. "Thank you, Miss Wales 1956," I said. "I'm eligible for another drink. Thanks, Trev; let's sit down."

Trevor turned appraising eyes towards me. "You need someone to help you lose a couple of stone. You are a bit taller than six foot, but I heard someone refer to you as chubby, the other day. You must be living on chips and beer."

I took out my cigarette case. "Have one of mine."

We both blew circles of smoke and watched them form a drifting pall.

"Actually, I'm a meat and two veg man," I said. "That's the way I was brought up. Some would say it's boring."

"Say no more – it's my custom too. Like father, like son. It's the same with your politics – it's parental influence at work. No, don't jump on me. I'm not knocking your dad. You've every reason to be proud of him.

"By the way, I heard your exchange of words with Malcolm. He's pathetic but vindictive, and in the pub every day. A big pal of the Weavers landlord."

"You mean Ugly Bill, as he's called behind his back. I know he used to be a follower of Sir Oswald

Mosley, but he looks a burned-out case now."

"Don't be too sure. You never know with those fellows. But what I want to know is, am I being called back to the army next week, or the week after? I was only a gunner in Essex –ended my National Service not long after you - and it'll be aircrew and parachutists they want, won't it?"

I smiled at his earnest manner. "Hell's bells, Trev, I am sure you will never fire a shot. The United Nations and the USA are against it and I shall be shell-shocked if the Labour Party doesn't demand a ceasefire."

"Let's leave it for now," said Margaret. "We've talked about it before and you know I disagree with you two. Let's hope that Nasser caves in now that we have shown we mean business. Trevor, tell Joe the gossip you heard about Kathleen.

"It's more than gossip, there's something you don't know about her, Joe. I've heard it at the bar from that girl who works in the general office. Jones is giving Kathleen another leg up, so to speak. What do you think of that?"

"Tell me more."

"She's going to be made head of a new Department of Communication Studies. There'll be no adverts, no interviews."

I tensed up, knowing that as Union chairman I would have to react to the challenge, but wondering how. "Bloody hell," I said, "even the people who always keep their heads down will tell us to do something about that - let alone those who are dyed in the wool Union men."

"But what can we do?" Trevor spoke with feeling. "We've been elected but we're not commanding officers. You're good at making your speeches, but I wonder how many would come to a protest meeting. They'd be too worried about their promotion prospects to put their heads above the parapets. Mind you, they'll resent the favouritism, especially when it's shown to a woman."

"I'm sick of the subject," Margaret said loudly. "Joe, there's something I want to ask you, if you don't mind. Do you think Julie will come back? I was really upset when she left you. Trev and I liked her a lot. Or should I mind my own business?"

"It's all right. It hurt me a lot. It all came out of the blue and vanished like smoke. She had grinned at me one lunch-time in The Weavers.

'I'm Julie'

'I'm Joe. Err... Let me get you a drink'

Her blue eyes gleamed under blonde, bobbed hair. We got talking and before long I knew her smile was a lasso pulling me towards her. We met in the pub again the next day and I no longer felt a loner for I knew I had a girlfriend only three years younger than I was.

Julie was enrolled on one of the Accountancy courses and that was why we married within six months, as a lecturer couldn't live openly in sin with a student. It was a Registry Office wedding, as neither of us was interested in churches

"Anyway, as you know, she moved in with me and it worked very well. She had a broad grin for everyone and you called her the star of last year's College dance. I was very happy with her, as she seemed to be with me, though my mother told me once she thought Julie wanted a more affluent, middle-class lifestyle.

"We went to dances, the cinema and the theatre and gave parties for our friends. We had a holiday in Brittany, where we thought we would like to buy a cottage one day.

"The question of having a child excited us both. Our talks about when this should happen – never if - always ended in warm embraces. I thought Julie should first complete her course and get a qualification, though she was not keen on working as an accountant. I liked her so much that my political interests took second place. But it all collapsed."

"What went wrong?"

" It's hard to say. Let's leave it at that."

Margaret held my hand in sympathy. "She was a lovely companion to all of us, but underneath she was just a visitor, who went back to where the Oklahoma grass was greener. Come on, Trev. We won't bother Joe with more questions. "It's a quickstep. You've drunk just enough to be able to do it. One more pint and you'd fall over."

I lit another cigarette, watching them swaying on the crowded floor. Not for the first time I had kept my emotions under the cover of nonchalance. Still, I should be on the floor myself. There's that girl drinking over by the bar. I've seen her at Union meetings and her figure is interesting, though I shan't get very close to it, now the band has gone into Rock 'n Roll.

47

CHAPTER 4

The storm clouds over Suez had gathered and finally burst, as the autumn advanced. It was Sunday morning, the day after the dance, and I was sipping tea in the buffet compartment of the train to Paddington, looking at the faded countryside flying by, and thinking glumly of the news from Hungary. I had turned on the World Service in the early hours and heard that Soviet tanks and a hundred thousand men had attacked Budapest.

They must have been preparing to go back in when they started pulling out, a week beforehand. It was very bad news. Also, five day ago Israel had invaded Egypt and Britain was obviously about to follow suit. Eden had gone crazy. Just then, as the train picked up speed after its stop at Oxford, I recognised a figure with a potbelly lurching down the corridor towards me. I had known Geoffrey well at university as a witty, debonair left-winger, an intellectual who could laugh at himself, as he did once when we were arguing with a belligerent, personally abusive Zionist. Drawing me from a likely brawl, Geoffrey remarked with a smile, "He would make me anti-Semitic, if I weren't a Jew."

He had always been very companionable. Now he said, "Hullo there, you look wonderful!"

I thought his outgoing charm was now less

natural, perhaps an affected style put on in dialogues with other important people, in Geoffrey's role as an economics advisor to British Rail. Perhaps his jovial look had a lacquer of complacency. I gave him an immediate political litmus test with a question about the Middle Eastern crisis.

Geoffrey answered smoothly: "I put Israel first every time. We owe it to the victims of the Holocaust. It's internationalism, Joe – and far more real than the pro-Soviet mantras we used to chant in our Oxford salad days."

"Even if the Israelis invaded in collusion with Eden?"

"There's no proof of that."

"It's coming into the light of day. What about the UN's call for a ceasefire and full withdrawal?"

"Not until there's agreement on international control of the Canal."

"So we carry on bombing and we start dropping paratroopers to kill even more Egyptians, while the rest of the world does nothing? You know, Geoff, I don't think the British lion roars as loudly today as you seem to think. Anyhow, I'm off to Trafalgar Square to the Law not War rally."

"Well, good luck to you, Joe. You haven't mentioned Hungary but we'll leave it to another time. Carol's here with me. I expect you knew we got married."

I nodded. "I hear she's a don at St Anne's." I remembered her as a miner's daughter, showing her feelings in her face and speech, which had the north Midlands accent, clipped and abrupt. She had jumped into the water fully clothed one May Day, which the Socialist Club was celebrating on the river.

As Carol entered the compartment, I was slightly surprised to see her wearing a hat but taken aback by her assured bearing and senior common room diction. When I asked her if she ever went back to the mining village, she flashed a smile and replied with a genteel drawl, "Oxford fully occupies me, except when we go to town for a concert, or have our holidays in France."

"Well, maybe not much wealth and power has been transferred to the miners and the other sons of toil, Carol, but you seem to be doing all right."

I was pleased that she blushed, and Geoffrey saved her from replying by his uproarious laughter, and his declaration, "We vote Labour, Joe."

"I'm sure you do. What are your career prospects?"

As they began to edge away to a table further down the compartment, Geoffrey paused and said they were keen Gaitskellites hoping to be given worthwhile jobs by the next Labour government.

"You know – a commission of enquiry for Carol and a senior admin post for me, as a temporary civil servant."

"So you must have made your peace with the Bomb then."

"It's not that simple. If the Russians have it, we have to as well. The logic's irresistible."

"Include me out. Anyhow, give my regards to any of the old crowd you come across, unless they're now Tories." My smile hid my dismay. Yesterday's friends had got off the socialist train.

My pulse quickened when I saw the demonstrators filling Trafalgar Square Banners fluttered, placards waved and even the lions seemed animated. Only Lord Nelson held himself aloof from the rabble that knew nothing of the Battle of the Nile.

Thinking it a good idea to have a pint before I found a place in the crowd, I walked away from the Square and came to a pub with a small smoking room, where I ordered a drink through a serving hatch separating the room from the bar. Three men wearing tweed jackets and cavalry twill trousers stood with their backs to me. They seemed to be comparing notes. One of them said, "My fellow has cooked his goose. I took a picture of him clapping one of the barmy army of platform speakers. He won't keep his job long in the Home Office, after I've sent it to the Permanent Secretary."

"Keep the volume down, old boy," one of the others said, turning his head to look over his shoulder. Immediately, he exclaimed, "I say, it's Joe, the odd man out. Remember him?"

They had been members of the rowing set at his college and their friendship had evidently lasted. "I suppose you're here to support the silver-haired Welsh hero of the hour," one of them said loudly."

"Right, first time. I haven't changed. It sounds as though you are here to take note of certain members of his audience."

"You are a consistent nigger in the woodpile, Joe. We'll give you that. I seem to remember when it was touch and go you whether you ended up in the College lake, one time after a Bumps supper."

51

The speaker with the finely honed vowels was Bob Dean, who had wanted to duck me but had failed to drum up support, although I wouldn't have minded if they had tried it on, as I had also been feeling reckless, after a drinking session at the Lamb and Flag with assorted political friends.

"I vaguely recall your proneness to delinquency," I said mildly. "What are you up to now? Are you full-time spies?"

"Rubbish. We're serving Queen and country in No 40 Commando Officer reservists. We could be part of the second or third wave of the invasion."

"I didn't know there'd been a first wave yet."

"You'll only have to wait a short while," Dean said, dropping his voice, as one of his friends gave a loud, cautionary cough.

"So you're holding the Empire together."

"We'll drink to that, and you must have one us. Your round, Leslie. He's Sir Leslie Bart, now, Joe. And then there's Anthony, the man with the cough."

He pointed to a very tall man, with dark, wavy hair and a brooding, slightly peevish expression. I nodded. It was Anthony who had loudly told off his scout for not laying a table in his room for a tea party. The middle-aged man had said, "Sorry, it won't happen again, sir," and had told me later that he was used to putting up with much more than that, as he had to keep his job, being too old for the car plant.

I had felt bound to propose a motion at a meeting of the Junior Common Room that college servants should be encouraged to join a trade union, and I smiled at the memory of the barracking and derisive cheers. It was different in personal relations, one to one. Anthony and his kind were so wreathed in good manners I had found it hard to fall out with them.

There were more pints in the pub, with laughs at my own well observed trips on the river in a punt, with female company. Anthony tilted at the eccentricities of some of the College Fellows:

"They should be made to get experience of a competitive, business environment. I have some sympathy with that brash Australian chap who complained to the College Provost that in philosophy tutorials they talked about everything except the matter they were supposed to be studying."

Leslie's voice seemed to droop like a basset hound's ears, as he barked, "Actual teaching was thought infra dig."

Bob roared out derisively, "It hardly mattered to you. You practically lived on the river, as I did. But you have a point. It's good to overhaul old traditions, so long as we preserve the ones that really matter."

"Such as?" I said.

We were on our third drink and the tone of the reply was challenging. Didn't you feel a buzz on Thursday, when you learned we'd knocked out all the wog bombers? You are an Englishmen, after all."

"I presume you mean 'Egyptian' bombers. What was there to feel excited about?

"It's prestige. We're still top dogs in most of Africa. We must keep hold of it. Don't you see that?

And, by the way, I don't need you to criticise my colloquial expressions."

"Perhaps you can do it yourself. But the main point is you'll have no prestige left when you have to turn tail. It's like a small college trying to be top dog on the river. Only it's much worse than that - it's like the others banding together to sink our boat."

Anthony's cultured, baritone voice rang out: "You really are a swine!" and lifted up his hand, holding half a glass of beer.

I managed to keep my composure. "You may be sorry if you pour that over me."

Obviously, Bob was also tired of fraternising with me. "Let me tell you something, Joe. Men of 3 Para will drop onto El Gmail airfield tomorrow. This is no time for talking like Lord Haw-Haw."

He grabbed my arm, but breaking free of the grip, I pushed him back over some chairs, before the others joined in. I taunted them, "What's happened to the social graces?"

Just then, a party of at least a dozen young people came streaming into the pub. "They're Empire Loyalists calling Bevan a bastard," I called out, as I felt a blow on the forehead from Anthony. I heard a scuffle and shouts but sat down, sore in the head and confused by the rapid turn of events. I looked up at a circle of sympathetic faces, and heard a young man say, "You're all right now. We left the rally for a quick drink. We soon turfed out those three fellows. We had the same odds against them as they had against you. You should have seen their bloody noses."

"I wish I had. I'm very glad you chose this pub.

My name's Joe."

"I'm Bryn. We've come down with this crowd from Swansea to support our man in Trafalgar Square. It's a bit like following the Welsh team Twickenham, especially as we've just beaten the English in a scrum. Oh, this is my sister, Jacky."

I saw a tallish woman wearing a poncho. She had dark eyes and full, well-shaped lips. She said in quite a deep tone, with the lilt of South Wales, "Your face is a bit discoloured on one side but you don't look too bad, boy."

I grinned and returned the compliment. She added that she had been in London for three years: "I am a town planner – I specialise in one way streets"

"All right. I'll watch how I go." I explained what I did and where I came from, while hoping they were come-on signals I was picking up from the lights in her eyes, the smile and the playful removal of the poncho, so as to expose her low-cut dress. Her hair was black, whereas Jenny's was fair, and she had a more single-minded manner, without Jenny's irony.

"Are you named after Joe Stalin?"

"That's right. I was born before he killed off many of his old comrades in the 'thirties."

"Well, even the best generals sacrifice thousands of lives to achieve their strategic aims. Talking about war, shall we go back to the Square?"

I held out my hand and she took it. I had a pleased, resigned feeling that she had taken a strong initiative. Here I go again. I stood behind her with my hands on her shoulders in the crowd, which shook like long grass in the wind as Bevan's shafts

55

were cheered. She pressed against my thighs, as the crowd pushed us closer together. A man in a duffel coat immediately in front of us jumped with enthusiasm and managed to turn to face us, exclaiming, not too grammatically, "Isn't it the greatest since Lloyd George's?"

We laughed together later on in a Lyons tea house, and she said that at the time of our close contact in the crowd my physical arousal was probably as big as Lloyd George's ever was. She made me an offer. "I'll make you a better cup of tea, if you like, and also bathe your bruise. It looks angrier now. I only live in Camden. I could even give you a ride to the station. I have a car, you know, though some men disapprove of my independence."

"I am all for equality – and yes, you can give me a cup of tea, and whatever else you like."

"Just you get to know me a bit better and you may not like what you find. I'm not like that stupid woman in the film- *A Kind of Loving*. She only wanted marriage. More like a kind of dying, I would say."

We were strolling away from the tea house, arm in arm, when two men in dark blue raincoats approached. One of them, who was sunburned and had a stiff, military bearing, said "Special Branch," and flashing an identification card said, "We believe you were in the George public house this afternoon, Mr Butler."

"That's right, I was. What's the problem? How do you know my name?"

"We should like to have a word with you alone, sir."

Jacky pressed my hand and walked some distance away. The sunburned man said, "We know a great deal about you. To keep to the point, you were talking in the pub about operational matters concerning Her Majesty's Armed Forces."

"No, you've got it wrong. I was informed that British forces will land in Egypt tomorrow. So what? It's hardly news."

I guessed that Dean and the others were taking revenge for their bloody noses, with the help of the police or MI5. They would have been part of the same surveillance team keeping an eye on the demo. All they had to do when they were thrown out of the pub was to make a phone call to get their friends to tail me.

"It's crazy. We aren't even at war. You can't stop my right of free speech."

I was trying to be calm but felt a surge of anger starting to make my speech less controlled. "What happens now? Do you take me to a windowless cell deep in the heart of Whitehall?"

"We could do something like that, if we thought it necessary, but we think you will be sensible. You have your job to consider. The publicity of an arrest would do no good to your career, to say the least. We are just here to warn you to tread carefully."

"Oh, get lost! Go back and tell your mates in 40 Commando that it's a lily-livered way to get their revenge for a drubbing."

The sunburned man gripped my arm and said, "You'd better shut your mouth, before I drop the polite conventions and show you what we can do to you. It's called action to restrain a suspect who resists arrest."

"Take your bloody hands off me!" I shouted, as he gave a hard pull to free his arm. I stood on the pavement outwardly aggressive in his posture and stare, but with a sinking feeling that I was being provoked into behaviour that would lead to an arrest.

"Listen to me, you scum," the sunburned man said. "When we want you, we shall get you, and it will be no picnic, believe me. Now fuck off."

I thought it was good advice. I turned and walked towards Jacky, who knew all the answers.

"Democracy? Is it hell! It's the iron hand of the state - for Queen and country!"

Later, we lay on her bed in a barely furnished room with white walls, on which a few prints hung. The whole flat had minimal decoration, which well suited her: "I had asthma in my teens and try to avoid surfaces where the dust can gather."

Everywhere was clean and a mere drop of tea on the low, wooden table in front of the sofa where we had sat moved her to fetch a cloth. She was no less brisk and efficient with sex. Her way was to undress immediately, as though we were long married, without the preliminary, sofa manoeuvres and gradual removal of clothes that excited me.

"No messing around, eh, boy? And, by the way, I use a Dutch cap."

Her figure was as good as the promise it had shown in the pub, and she presented her breasts for caresses, as a child expects to be patted on the head.

"That's the pleasure zone," she commented, "for women as well as men," and I almost fancied she mentioned an admission charge. She motioned for me to come inside her and soon my performance was over and we lay there, while my body tingled as I recalled Jenny's vibrant touch.

readily have her again. I assumed her feeling for me was as clinical, and was relieved when she put it into words:

"That was a nice screw, Joe. I think a sexual relationship should leave you with a warm glow, which gradually fades over time. It shouldn't cause sorrow or regrets. It's complete in itself. I have to tell you something, however, and it may embarrass you. Cut your fingernails before we make love again."

"You must know you're a very forthright woman."

"That's because I don't let social conventions stay in the way of my natural impulses. The equality of the sexes should be part of every socialist's thinking. Unfortunately it's not. But it will be, one fine day. Now, about that policeman."

She moved my hand away from her leg as I was turning to embrace her again, and said, "I was just thinking you could write a letter to the papers. It's a civil liberties issue."

"Perhaps we could both sign it."

She flushed. "I didn't witness your argument with the three men in the pub. You can tell the whole story."

I was amused but made no comment on her instinct for self-protection, as I wrote an account of the incident and then spent a long time making five copies for posting that night to the national daily papers. I would look at the papers in the public library for the next three days, not really expecting my letter to be published. Nor was it. She asked rather tensely when I would ring her.

"I don't know. In a week or two's time, if you like."

"What do you mean, 'if I like'? You gave a good impression of liking me, just now. I'm not an old cardigan that you can pick up or put down as you fancy."

I looked at her white face and staring eyes and thought how a minute ago she had seemed to imply it would be easy to part. I felt a slight shiver of apprehension. Would the ground give way beneath my feet again? Julie's face came to me in a flash and stayed with me on the slow train home.

CHAPTER 5

She said she would like to visit her father in America, the land of her birth. I thought it natural that she should want to see him again, especially after the loss of her mother.

"I'm a city girl at heart – four weeks of country life will be enough for me."

She often talked about the white house with the mailbox at the end of the striped lawn, and behind it the endless plains of corn and grass, under the immense blue sky.

No memory of our two-year marriage is as sharply etched as her return from the States. It was a day in May. I awoke at dawn, hearing the alarm but lying doggo under the blankets, before stretching my arms and legs sensually and daydreaming of Julie. I pulled the covers off slowly, edged out of bed and switched on the light. Usually I gave a quick glance in the wall mirror, but as I was alone I stood up straight, patted down my light wavy hair and eyed my paunch, wondering if she would still like me in a few years' time, if I became really fat.

Half an hour later I was driving my pre-war Morris 8 through the early morning mist hanging over the A road leading south from our Birmingham home. The white jackets on the saplings planted on a grassy slope shimmered in the half-light like graveyard crosses waving an invitation.

As I drove through Oxfordshire, the day was at least faintly blue and streaked with pale sunshine. I stopped for a couple of minutes, lowered the window and listened to the 6 am news summary of world reactions to Nasser's threat to nationalise the Suez Canal. I didn't blame the Egyptians. Not many of them would ever fly like Julie on the Super Constellation. The so-called affordable transport for the masses was strictly for the privileged West. Even here it was mainly for the rich, but we had saved enough to pay for her ticket. I thought the flight was almost historic as jets would replace propellers before long.

I entered London Airport, a few minutes after the Pan Am flight had arrived early from New York. Some of the travellers looked as crumpled as newspapers and chocolate wrappers littering the floor tiles, while others seemed jittery as dogs waiting to be released from a strays' compound. I wasn't surprised they were done for. It was a twenty-hour flight and they keep topping them up with free food and drink, so they're bound to be comatose.

I scanned the concourse until I saw Julie sitting slumped against her luggage. She seemed duly worn out by the flight, for she was limp in my arms and unresponsive to my embrace and first, light kiss. I thought I should hold back from smoothing her dark brown hair, no longer compact or shiny. I wanted to touch the light stubble of her eyebrows and push a finger between the broad, soft lips, until she bit hard and I wailed in playful pain. It seemed better to wait.

Later our cheeks would touch and her tired face would light up in the famous Julie grin.

"Let's go home," I said, and she nodded.

As she rose to her feet, straightening her navy shirt, I looked at her American blue jeans. She had worn a skirt for her departure.

"They're glamorous – they really suit you."

Her good looks showed some colour when I spoke but she stayed silent. When we had gathered speed on the open road I started speaking in a mock American drawl

"Well, I'll be darned! Sure glad to have you back. How was your daddy? I guess he loved seeing his little girl after all those years away from her.

I slowed down as we came to a village and wound down the window slightly, enough to let in the sound of Bill Haley and the Comets rocking around the clock. It stopped my banter, which had been prompted by a feeling of unease at Julie's silence. We passed a few lorries but the commuter traffic was still sparse. Several army trucks went by towards London and I wondered if they were getting ready for the showdown, if Egypt took over the Canal.

I could see the sun was taking its time to dry the legs of a concrete bridge, and the road had a damp, matt finish. It was not hot but Julie's neck was damp. "You look as sticky as though you've ben cleaning the bathroom and cooking for a party at the same time."

I tried to set her at ease with more small talk. "I always find it hard to remember the name of the guy who's playing Shylock at Stratford, this season. I've booked seats for Stratford. Is that all right?"

She nodded in reflex action. A minute later I put my hand on her knee and thought of pulling up for a moment to kiss her. She pulled away from me, as she bent to take a handkerchief from her handbag. She said nothing and I looked at her bowed head. There was something wrong. I had never known her so hangdog. At the same time I was distracted by the sunshine flooding the windscreen and dazzling both of us. I braked hard, causing the car to swerve, turn a half circle and shake from side to side. The side of my face slammed against the steering wheel. Julie was thrown forward, her raised arms hitting the dashboard.

I was sick with fear that she had been hurt. I grabbed the wheel, started up and drove on to a grass verge. She seemed barely bruised and so I dabbed my cut face with a handkerchief, with a surge of disappointment when she did not offer to help me.

"Let's talk when we get home," she said. I glanced at her. She was poker-faced. I nodded so as to delay the blow that I felt was coming. When I took another quick look, she was beetroot red and gripped her handbag like a lifebelt. Drained of all elation, I wondered what was wrong. The cheerful fantasy of the drive down had gone with mist. The saplings looked plain and gawky in the bright light.

But I was my usual controlled self as carried her case into the apartment. She sat down at once and spoke in a low but firm tone.

"Joe, I met someone else. He's called Dave. He's divorced and I am going to live with him. I shall be with a man who I really love."

The pressure within her was released. Her face became contorted and the tears flowed, but I felt that she was happy. My anger rose. It seemed unreal. We had hardly ever had a row and I had never hit her.

'Tell me what happened. How long have you known this man?'

"I only knew him for three days but I knew at once I wanted to spend the rest of my life with him"

"Three days! You' sound like a cool, unfeeling two-timer transferring your affection and loyalty so very easily – as though all the time you're just playing a part"

. The words flowed out of her. 'Oh Joe, don't be so offensive and out of character. Oklahoma is all I ever wished for. No one's hustling you. You have all the time and space you want in the world. You know how the sun in England is changeable and lifeless most of the time? I was brought back to life by the flaring sun in Oklahoma. We used to thresh through the grass mixed with foxtails. It was beautiful at dusk too, with the red streaks in the sky, the long call of the doves and the faint whisper of the wings of the screech owl.

'Dave parked his high-mounted pickup by the roadside and left his keys in the ignition. 'They'll still be there when we get back,' he said. 'Over here, the folks go out and leave their doors unlocked." Dave said I could be a real American housewife, spending the morning meeting my girlfriends, reading a few books and helping his mother with the supper.

'I loved the Cherokee people I met in the market. They thought I had descent from them, if not pure blood. Pa told me that when I was a small child'

I had heard the story from her before. She had the colouring and the severe but vulnerable look that stares from the pages of the Indian history books. She had pictures +of the Cherokees' art and stories of their life in the Tennessee Mountains, before they were driven down the Trail of Tears to Oklahoma.

"'I was an Okie with an English accent - quite a celebrity wherever I went, listening to Cajun music, whenever I could.'

I imagined her dream mood, deepened by the monotonous beat of the music. It was like listening to a convert to a religious cult.

"Why the hell did you bother to come back?"

"Because I owed it to you, Joe. I had to tell you to your face. It has been two good years. I did love you. You have principles. You are not selfish or materialistic."

"Don't preach at me! You thought it all out. The truth is you knew I would track you down in the Bible belt and cause a stir there, if you didn't come home."

I had felt bothered by her words, "not materialistic." We would never have lived in a mansion but our rooms were spacious and quite stylish in decor. There were certainly no boundless acres of green and golden country; the ring road was nearby, sometimes roaring like the sea. But inside the apartment, the large paintings radiated warmth. Another room was lined with bookshelves but I remembered her saying ruefully that the books were nearly all mine. I looked at one of the paintings, which showed Puck casting a spell on a sleeping girl. It seemed prophetic, except that the scene was the leafy banks of Warwickshire, instead of the plains of Oklahoma.

Julie took a bath and pulled the shower curtain across when I came to the doorway. When she brushed past me, swathed in towels, her lips were as enticing as when I had met her at the airport. She went into the kitchen and asked me if she could have an egg from the fridge.

I shouted, "What sort of question is that? You stocked it up only a month ago. You can have the whole bloody contents if you want to. You could live as my wife for a few weeks, while we talked this thing through. I had no idea that the marriage was so stale to you. Why couldn't you have been open with me? What about the love note you left on my pillow before we left for the airport? What about the one you sent from Oklahoma? Did they mean nothing?"

"Joe, I didn't foresee what took place. I only knew I was going to see family. Don't ask me to explain what happened. I only know that the moment I saw Dave, he was the man I wanted to be with'"

Her tone was weak and high pitched. I thought I could hear a little girl saying, "Go away! You are not my best friend any more. I have a new best friend."

"'OK. If it's what you want, just go.'"

She filled another suitcase and called for a taxi, like a holidaymaker at the end of her stay. As she left, my body tensed up and I almost screamed in protest. Later I wished I had been able to make a better job of breaking down my customary reserve. I lay listlessly in my armchair for hours, imagining the Cherokee girl on the trail to a white house in the golden country under a sky always clear blue I longed for her, as the light began to fade and my books and pictures shone faintly.

I thought she would be content out there for a while, until the colours seemed less bright and she could see the fault lines. She was rejecting me and reaching out for an illusion. Or perhaps it was real. In time she would know. I was not so different from her. Perhaps I was just as starry-eyed. What an irony! Except that the mystique that had gripped me from early childhood was not America. It was another country, but unlike Julie I had never been to my utopia.

After dozing on the train, I was in bed by 2 am, though I turned and shifted about for a long time, trying to relax. What a week it had been! Was life as difficult for my parents? They had been united by great causes, but they hadn't saved Spain or
stopped Hitler. These days, Suez is less stirring because it's only about a useless attempt to save a dying empire. Also, the political choices have become a bit clouded over. The Soviet Union is being judged on its strong-arm tactics in Hungary and whether it's really a superior system, now that things are so much improved in the capitalist West. Nevertheless, I still had the marks of the parental stamp. Time would tell whether they would wear off.

CHAPTER 6

The next morning I ran up the stone steps of one of the cluster of Victorian buildings, admiring the solid woodwork, patterned floor tiles and windows edged with stained glass.

Jones had an open-door policy which allowed him to spend two or three hours every day chatting to whoever came along. I switched my thoughts back to his supposed affair with Kathleen. It could be just a product of fevered speculation. If it really existed, it was discreet. No one had even seen them holding hands. The only evidence that it was happening was her rapid advancement from clerk to personal secretary, to Office Studies lecturer. It would be suicidal to hint at it to the Principal. He was a charmer in his forties but a tough opponent, with an opportunism that owed something to his war service in submarines. Gerry Jones made up the rules as he went along, saying "Once you have been stuck on the bottom of the sea, nothing else matters very much."

"Come in, Joe," he said cheerfully. "Come in and have a noggin. Sorry to hear about your domestic upset."

"Thanks. That puts it diplomatically. Still, it's not like being stuck on the bottom of the ocean in a big cigar case."

The Principal laughed and nodded vigorously. He was sleekly dressed in a grey woollen suit, with a challenging red tie matching his eyes and cheeks. I was fully prepared for flattery and charm laced with hints of promotion, but changing to cold formality if our wills openly clashed.

Jones said, with studied casualness, as he poured out two measures of whisky, "Don't you think that some of those Arts people in Academic Studies should be transferred to the hulk? They are stuffing the minds of their students with anti-establishment propaganda. Someone put up a poster supporting Nasser."

"The lecturers are trying to make their students think. They don't deserve the worst building in the college. That should be closed down or perhaps given to the Accountants."

"Very funny. I knew you would defend them. You are all kith and kin, standing up for the enemies of the British Empire. I often wonder why I went to war. All the low life of the Middle East and Africa has made this country a laughing stock. We should have called back the wartime army to show the likes of Mossadeq and the Mau-Mau who were the masters. And now look at this latest humiliation."

"I keep politics out of the lecture room, but if you're asking, I am all for Nasser taking over the Canal. He needs the revenue to build the dam which the Americans were going to pay for until they broke their promise."

"I've no time for the Yanks. Eisenhower's not to be trusted. But the Egyptians will make a balls-up of running the Canal, just you see."

"And suppose they don't?"

"We'll have it back off them, anyway. You'll have a rough time in College now that we've gone to war and you still shout out your Egyptian propaganda. There are too many men here who fought for this country, not many years ago."

"That was for a worthwhile cause."

Jones shook his head, but I left it at that. I thought he might even look for a reason to sack me. I was being led on and had to beware of answering back angrily. A break-up and the suspension of meetings might suit him.

So I said, with as artless a smile as I could produce, "What about the whales then?" Shouldn't we end the slaughter?"

This time, it was the Principal who took the bait. His voice rose: "You must be joking. The oceans are full of whales. I saw enough in the South Atlantic to last me a lifetime."

After pouring two tots of whisky, he said in a quiet, winning tone, "What can I do for you, Joe?"

I braced myself. Mention of Kathleen directly would detonate an instant row and achieve nothing. An appeal to the Board of Governors would then be the only resort, to be avoided if possible, since they were on the friendliest of terms with Jones.

Mr Jones shot up in his chair and said brusquely, "Organisation of the college is my affair, not the Union's. Joe, we shall be looking for a new head of Academic Studies before long. You know old Jim is retiring this year. The job would be just up your street - you're his unofficial deputy already. Nobody is better qualified and it's not as big and

71

burdensome as some of the others. You could do it, young as you are."   He paused and then added, "Although you would hardly have time to be Union chairman as well as head of department."

I had to smile at the effrontery of the man. It was a bribe put straight on to the table by someone who had no need of finesse. Yet I realised I half-wanted to accept it. "I'd love to be in charge, doing things my way."

Mr Jones gave me a broad grin signalling that he understood the dilemma. Then he changed the subject. "I think the refectory should stay open another hour or two in the evening. They say the best discussions take place in the extended tea breaks, especially with the works managers."

"I'll support that," I said warmly, knowing how easy it would be for me to court popularity with Mr Jones. As long as he kow-towed, I'd get on well with him. Next thing, he'd be made Vice-Principal. That evening, I told Trevor about the insipid fantasy and we both laughed, as we went to our classes.

The topic for the evening was housing in the public sector. My presentation of the issues was well received by the serious-minded group of adult students. In the discussion, a middle-aged customs official, a strong supporter of the free market, was pitted against his usual opponent, the socialist owner of an old-established lock firm.

They first locked horns over Suez, the customs man wishing he could be called up for service and his opposite number saying it was easy for someone well above the maximum age for enlistment to have heroic fantasies.   Then a fierce   argument over subsidies involved everyone, and at the end I felt I had given them their money's worth.

The next day I drove with Trevor to a hotel in Solihull for a meeting of Union officers. The prospect of a talk by the regional official about the equal pay campaign seemed dull.

"All he'll have to say can be read in the pamphlet that we were sent a month ago," said Trevor. "I don't know why we're pressing this one so hard. The The principle has already been agreed with the Government. It's coming in by stages. But it's bloody ironic, since no-one will benefit more than you know who."

Outside the hotel, a few bulbous Jaguars and a Sunbeam Talbot jostled for space with cars of lower status, such as Ford Anglias and Morris Minors, all looking new.

"The Jags look good," Trevor remarked. "There's one over there with a small space next to it. Your Morris 8 should fit into it."

Inside, a few people that they recognised as Union men from other colleges, stood by the bar, but the dominant conversation came from a crowd of middle-aged men reclining on fawn settees, sipping their shorts. One of them, fleshy and self-assured, jabbed the air vigorously with his fingers to reinforce his various assertions. "There's a shortage of labour in industry – it's in the civil service. The bureaucrats are holding us back, with their regulations about what we can and cannot do. The only thing that will pull us together as a nation is putting down the wogs who want to take over our Canal."

"What utter drivel," I muttered to Trevor, who sniffed the pervasive odour of brandy and said, "The small-time fat cats know how to spend their afternoons. This is real management practice."

"It seems a bit remote from college theory, Joe."

. "They wouldn't think twice about promoting their secretaries."

After buying two halves, I joined Trevor on a window seat. I mused about Mr Jones. Perhaps I'm getting the Principal's sins out of proportion. The man just sees himself as another industrial manager, like the fellows in front of the bar and he deserves some sympathy since he'd been in the war. Still, Jones is in the wrong, though what the Union can do about it is a problem.

I didn't like to think my behaviour was ordained and that I had to follow the political lodestar of my parents. I was an instinctive trade unionist, as they had been, and I had followed their lead, in cherishing a Marxist vision of a better society called socialism. The sensible thing would have been to join the Labour Party, and criticise it from within instead from outside. Sometimes I daydreamed about how well I might have got on by now, if I had. Perhaps I still would join. Still, life at the college wasn't bad. I knew I could say what I liked to anyone, if pushed hard enough.

"It's time for the meeting. Come on, Trev."

We made their way down a long corridor to the meeting room, where the regional official spoke about common justice for female teachers. Commenting on how few women were at the meeting, I said in the discussion that true equality was a long way off.

When tea was served, I left the room cautiously and returned to the bar, leaving Trevor talking. It was not closing time yet, and many of the businessmen were still holding forth under a shroud of smoke. After downing a brandy and chaser, I set off down the corridor towards the meeting, looking for a Gents sign, at first casually and then with growing impatience, as I passed room after room. The discomfort became insistent, as I swivelled into a side passage and came to a few more featureless doors.

I turned the handle of the last one casually, not expecting it to open but it did and I felt a rush of gratitude towards someone for not locking it. I rushed into the room, but froze at an unnerving sight. There was Kathleen in a blue slip, and Mr Jones wearing only underpants. I stuttered, "Sorry."

The Principal stared at me but was almost equal to the occasion, as Kathleen ran into the bedroom.

"As you see, Joe, you bloody interloper, Tuesday afternoon is the time when I try to enjoy some academic freedom. Unfortunately, we were in too much of a hurry to make sure that the key was properly turned in the lock. I suppose you came to that damned Union conference, which I only found out was on when we got here."

"Can I use your lavatory?"

"So that's why you burst your way in. Yes, it's over there."

When I got back to the room, Kathleen was sitting on the couch, fully clothed, hunched up and pink with embarrassment. I saw smudged make-up and eyes looking vacant and slightly stupid. I thought she had no allure and looked the part of the Principal's woman, paid for out of public funds. Fantasy time was over. No matter what the cost, I'd fight this appointment. In the last resort, I'd go to the local paper and cry scandal.

Just then, Mr Jones came in, dapper in his grey suit, as ebullient as ever. "So then, Joe, is your number two outside?"

"Yes, he's there." The answer was an overstatement, as Trevor would be drinking tea in the hall, but I saw that it could be very useful to him if Jones were to believe that a second witness was at hand.

"Strange thing is I was just mentioning the matter of the Academic Studies headship that came up at our meeting this morning. Have you thought any more about it?"

"Well, yes, I'd love to have it. I could make it the cultural heart of the town."

"Really! Tell me how you would irrigate the desert."

"We should make it a real arts centre for the community. I should make my staff feel that their opinions and experience were listened to. I would remember that there are lots more people out there who left school at fourteen and deserve a shot at higher education."

"Ever the idealist, Joe."

"I know it's just a dream, because the price is too high. I'd have to go along with Kathleen's promotion

76

and apart from that, how could I accept a job that other people didn't even have a chance to apply for?

Kathleen butted in. "I have something to say, Gerry. I'm no longer considering the new post. It would be too stressful. I should always think of Joe seeing us in here and looking down his nose at me."

Mr Jones scowled at me, but said calmly, "So that's it, my boy. The lady says no, although she's an ambitious and very capable person. And what will you do? Tell the world what you have seen? I think you are too much of a man to do that. You should apply for the headship when old Jim goes. It will be advertised. I shan't bother with the Department of Communication Studies."

His old buccaneer manner had fully returned, as though what had happened was not too important when he thought of his submarine on the bed of the Atlantic, with the oxygen running out. I knew it was time to go, taking my winnings with me, knowing I would never apply for a job in which I had to give up his Union work and be dependent for support and departmental funds on the mercurial moods of Jones. Saying simply, "Your personal relations are not my business, and I shan't broadcast anything I may have seen," I gave a nod and left the room. I assumed Jones would be vengeful and that there would be trouble ahead. But a victory in the short term was very pleasurable.

The meeting had just ended and Trevor was waiting outside the room.

"Where have you been, Joe?"

"I met Jones – he was drinking with the managers. We had a useful conversation in which he said he wouldn't be going ahead with the new department."

"You don't sound as though you're joking, Joe. I don't know how you managed it. There must be more to it than you've let on. Union success on this magnitude is almost unbelievable. You'll be saying next he's given you Kathleen, as well."

"No, I'm not kidding you, and no she's not the one for me. Jones and Kathleen are two of a kind – charming and cunning. I need someone on my wave length, as barmy as me."

"You may be unconventional, you may be an extremist like your parents – or their influence on you may be slipping away -- but you're not barmy. Anyhow, Julie could still come back."

"No chance. It wouldn't work if she did. I need someone right for me. I doubt if I'll find anyone. "

We drove home and talked about Aston Villa's chances in the new season.

CHAPTER 7

The next morning, the black, stone façade of the college glistened after an early shower. Some students from Hong Kong and Malaysia, who stood smoking by the door, nodded to me as I skipped up the steps into the entrance hall looked over by the large portrait of my partial namesake and the college's patron, Joseph Chamberlain.

The Management Accountancy students who came to me for Economic Principles were mostly slumped in their seats, in various stages of wakefulness, though some of them were alert enough to ask questions.

A man of about twenty-five already had the parchment complexion of a middle-aged company accountant. "Sir", he said, "how serious was the fall in the gold and dollar reserves reported in the news?"

"Very serious. Washington refused to give economic assistance, and the Russians threatened to use force. Eisenhower's threat was the more serious. The reserves could have gone into free fall as the military situation developed. No wonder the Cabinet has voted for a ceasefire."

"That's a defeatist attitude, isn't it?" a girl said angrily, shaking her shoulder-length blonde hair. "What about the sacrifices of our boys?"

The Chinese girl student called Li rarely spoke up but now answered in ringing tones, "The old colonial rule is over, can't you understand?"

I moved hastily to close the discussion, before it got out of hand. If the strong emotions still swirling round the nation poured into my lecture room, news of the political row would soon get round the College and it could be awkward if I had to explain it to the Principal. I said firmly, "I was just stating the facts and the predictions of many commentators. Whether it's good or bad is for you to judge. Now let's turn to the business of the day."

I was not sure whether she was trying to help me, when Li spoke up again.

"Sir, is it your opinion that we can ever have certain knowledge of the world around us?"

I was taken aback, and a ripple of laughter ran through the class. The girl was delicately pretty, and a bright white blouse offset very well her dark, wavy hair. I wondered if she was engaging me in conversation because she fancied me, or if her question was perhaps a diversion from tariffs and trade. But she was too conscientious a student to want to do that. I concluded it was Li's attempt to cool the temperature that she had helped to raise.

I hesitated before replying, "Well, this is one way to wake up in the morning. I'll do my best. You may have heard of Bishop Berkeley."

"Yes, sir, I learned about him in my studies in Hong-Kong. A town in California is named after him."

"Well, then, he believed there's no material world existing independently of minds. Colours, shapes, smells, tastes, sense of touch – all these are perceptions imprinted on our minds by the great creator. The trouble is, we don't think like that in everyday life."

When someone called out, "Don't jump, we're not that bad," and a fat young man from the Black Country interrupted with, "Oi believe in Fair-ther Christmas," I thought I had successfully steered the group away from politically loaded questions, until, as the laughter had died down, the girl said, "That sounds like something Karl Marx might have said, sir."

I felt he had to respond to the challenge of her question: "It could be as you say, though it's not only Marxists who reject the notion that all that exists is the mind of God and the minds that he has created."

A cheer went up from the back of the room and someone called out, "Didn't Marx play for the Villa in 1889?"

"No, that was Cinderella, but she was no good at football, because, as I expect you are all aware, she ran away from the ball."

The collective groan that arose was what I had reckoned on. The atmosphere was lightened, and I could now get on with the lesson in the theory of opportunity costs. Soon I saw them all furiously taking notes.

Li came up to me as the students were streaming out of the room and I warmed to her friendly grin, partly covered by her long, limp hair. Looking at her long legs and narrow waist, I asked if she had been a dancer.

"I went to ballet lessons," she said, "but it is not

81

rewarding financially, unless you are brilliant. If I become an accountant, there is good opportunity for me to earn enough to repay my parents. They had to borrow money to finance my education. We used to live in Malaya, but during the fighting, my father managed to get us into Hong Kong, to stay with members of the family."

"Well, you certainly ask some unusual questions in class."

"They interest me. I hope they did not embarrass you. While I am in this country I want to ask educated people many questions that are not in the textbooks of Accountancy."

She was looking at me very intently and I warmed to her sincerity. "It's all right," I said. "No one seemed to mind. I'd like to know what you think of my answers."

"I agree with you. I think also that when you referred to fairies at the bottom of the garden, you were thinking of the gods that people worship."

"Well. No, I wasn't, but since you ask, I don't believe in a Supreme Being. I think very few people do, in their heart of hearts."

"Neither do I. But tell me, if you leave out God, how you explain civilisation?"

"Basically in material terms - technological changes bringing in new economic structures, with new social classes, immense improvements in people's lives but also new international conflicts that have led to our world wars and the atom bomb. I believe we need socialism in order to control the material power produced by science and technology.

There you are – that's the lecture that I couldn't deliver to the students, this morning"

She clapped her hands but said, "It sounds a very automatic process, like going up in a lift, from capitalism to socialism."

"No, it's up to people to choose.   You know that the Revolution in China didn't just happen."

"No, the people decided which side they were on," she said assertively. "China will move the world one day. Perhaps you should go there yourself. You could teach English and wear a khaki tunic."

"Perhaps I will, especially if I have friends to help me," I said.   She laughed loudly, and I issued a general invitation for her to bring some of her friends for a meal at my home, saying I'd take a snapshot of them with the Matisse women.   We exchanged addresses and shook hands.

Late in the afternoon I was entering the staff car park, thinking how good it was to have friends amongst the students.   The Morris was looking less and less desirable, as I visualised the pea-green Standard Ten, that I'd trade it in for at the end of the month. Still, the old black thing shouldn't be leaning to one side, as though it had had a stroke. Then I saw that both tyres on the driver's side were flat. I had never known anyone victim of a practical joke like that.

I had a spare wheel, which I fitted, but I couldn't pump up the other tyre. I picked up the wheel and got someone to give me a lift to a garage, where the puncture was repaired while I waited. But I had to lug the wheel with me to a bus back to the college, and then fit it on the car, so that felt weary and angry by the time I set off home to cook sausage and mash.

The next morning I found the windscreen had a jagged hole, the upholstery was torn, and SHIT was scratched on the bonnet. More crude lettering on the side of the car said, 'Next time it's you.'

I called the police, but they said there were always young hooligans about and it was just unfortunate the car had been outside near the road, all night.

"Don't you think it was related to the earlier business with the tyres?" I said, but they shrugged it off, with "Sorry, sir, what can we do?"

I admitted to myself they didn't seem to have much to go on, and Trevor's view was that it was probably just one of those days when coincidences happened, as though they were part of an overall plan that didn't really exist. "It never rains but it pours," Joe. "In a week's time you'll hardly remember it. I'm sorry about the expense. Are you comprehensively insured?"

"Yes, but I shan't claim. It wouldn't be worth it. I wasn't getting much for it in exchange for the Standard. Now, it'll be scrap prices."

I thought Trevor might be right and that I shouldn't exaggerate the significance of my troubles, but still felt tense when I drove home from the garage, after a new windscreen had been fitted to the old car, and black paint brushed over the graffiti.

Then I found a note pushed into the letterbox, with a few words scrawled on it: *Go back to Russia.*

I thought I'd better start looking over my shoulder, especially if there was a group of fellows in the street. .I thought of the malevolent mood of the fellow lecturer Malcolm, at the College dance. But he was not the bold type;   it was even more unlikely that it was someone from the Management Accountancy class.

The next morning I drove to College, where I saw a similar slogan, with my name on it, white-washed across the wall by the entrance.   I also saw, with a great surge of relief, Li and another Chinese girl starting to scrub it off.

"I'm sorry, Mr Butler. This should not happen," said Li. "I do not know why anyone should want to attack you in this way. We will clean the brickwork. The Principal, Mr Jones, came down to see this rubbish. I told him I was going to ask the members of our Economics group to sign a letter to him, stating that you are an excellent teacher and we condemn this attempt to discredit you."

"Thank you," I answered softly, feeling too numbed to express my gratitude more warmly, thinking I'd like to kiss each of them on the cheek, but it would probably be unwise, as they might draw the right conclusions.

"It's very good of you," I said. "You have to remember that before the war Oswald Mosley was a Parliamentary candidate, not very far from here."

"Why is that relevant, Sir?" asked Li.

"Well, Mosley used the rhetoric of racial prejudice to appeal to people, especially amongst the most depressed social groups, who found it easier to blame Jews for social problems than to look for their real causes. Such people today might well be responsible for acts of vandalism. The Suez War could easily whip up their hatred for Arabs and for people who are opposed to the war."

When I entered the staff room, the hubbub stopped and some of my colleagues looked away, but others came to meet me, including Trevor, who said, "Joe, this is bloody ridiculous. I think Jones should call in the police. It's his college that has been defaced and his member of staff that's been insulted."

As he spoke, there was a phone call from Jones, asking to see me immediately.   The Principal was relaxed as he sat drinking coffee, knowing he had the advantage, because I was the accused. He was enjoying the prospect of the encounter.

"What's all this about, Joe?" Jones said cheerfully.

"Some right-wing idiot's trying to stir up prejudice against me."

"Hold on, name-calling isn't going to help. The first question is about what you've been up to lately, so as to provoke these expressions of dislike."

"I don't understand you. Are you condoning these slogans on your walls?"

"You see," Jones said, ignoring the question and leaning over in what seemed to me a falsely confidential manner, "I heard from a little bird that you took the bit between your teeth in class yesterday and gave a lecture on Marxism, as well as attacking the Government's Suez policy while our troops are in action. Is that true?"

"Absolutely not. What's going on? Who's been ringing you up?"

My thoughts were racing from one suspicion to another. Perhaps it was the fellow in the class who joked about Father Christmas.

"You must surely understand, Joe, that political detachment is of the highest importance in teaching."

"I know that and approve of it. I don't talk politics to my students; I stick to the syllabus. I made an objective comment on the Suez situation, in answer to students' questions."

"Is Marxism part of your syllabus?"

"I made a passing reference, also in answer to a question put by a student. It took far less time than many lecturers spend talking about the local football team. The subject of the Economics lecture was well covered in the time."

I felt the blood rush to my face, as I became more emphatic, but Jones stayed relaxed and said, "We'll see how it goes. I gather that some of your student friends are rubbing the whitewash off the front wall. Tell them they needn't write to me on your behalf. You aren't in trouble, but watch what you're about."

As I turned on my heel I reckoned my rebuttal of the charges had been good enough to cause him to back away from considering a possible confrontation with the college governors. The reaction of a body of mixed political composition couldn't be prejudged with any degree of assurance. could well champion freedom of the individual, rather than opt for a witch-hunt.

I saw Li later on in the refectory. "I am very pleased that you are all right," she said in a tone that I knew

showed real concern for me. I felt glad of her
 sympathy and almost put my hand on her arm. But
 if I did that, I could be making a fool of myself. She
was a serious-minded person, never mind her liquid
eyes and full lips. I was further relieved I had
behaved properly when she spoke of her boyfriend
studying Engineering. "It is good," she said, "to have
friends with whom you can talk about things you
have in common. It doesn't matter whether they are
women or men."

   I saw the slight amusement in her eyes as she
spoke, and knew that after reading my mind she was
telling me that I had behaved correctly. Well, fancy
that! I had actually made a woman friend, on the
same terms as I had men friends. What would
Granddad have thought of it?

CHAPTER 8

My invitation to spend Boxing Day at Trevor's came while the two of us were out jogging along the river bank, where boulders and large tufts of coarse grass made the going heavy.

"We should do it once a week, until the snow falls," Trevor said, breathing noisily, "to get rid of your paunch and clear my chest. I'm giving up smoking."

"Oh, yeah."

"Honest. Margaret thinks it might cause cancer. Dad died of it in his fifties."

I tried in vain to keep up with the winter debris speeding by on the stream, as the wind flapped my shorts against my knees and blew the cold into my eyes. I was happy to go to Trevor's, riding on the seasonal tide of sociability, like one of the leaves in the current.

As we made our way back to my car, I resolved to suggest to Jacky that she drove up from Swansea on Boxing Day morning. She was probably available and that meant a lot, despite her emotional swings, as the prospect of being single at Christmas was unappealing. If she got on all right with Margaret, the two men would be free to drink and talk. It'd be couples again, with one new woman. And then, to be honest, there was the sex.

I spent Christmas Day quietly at my mother's house, drinking Co-op tea and listening to Paul Robeson records, including the *Song of the Steppes*, which stirred me as much as when I heard it in the war.

Jacky had accepted my invitation and arrived late the following morning, in her humpback Anglia. Kissing me heartily, she said she had found my place without any trouble. "No problem for a town planner."

She looked carefully at the large, cream settee, which was crossed by a band of sunshine, and at the bright pictures on the walls, before giving her verdict: "I like it. But I'm not one of those Matisse models, passively playing the mandolin for your pleasure. I'm a woman who interferes and stirs things up. If you look in the mirror, you'll see I've already made my mark on you."

I grumbled, when I saw the imprint of her lipstick on my cheek. Bursting into loud laughter, she exclaimed, "You're like a sheep daubed by the farmer. Well, if I'm your owner, I can put a crook round your neck and take into the bedroom any time I please."

"You can do what you like, later on, but it's time we set off. They were expecting us half an hour ago."

It was my first sight of the new bungalow Trevor had moved into, a few weeks earlier. I liked the neat semi, with large windows and detached garage, to which the frost still clung. Inside, the bare walls, painted orange in the hall and primrose in the lounge, were relieved by fawn rush matting on the floors and a few pieces of furniture in beech.

Helen Shapiro was singing *Tip-Toe through the Tulips* on a Dansette, which Margaret said she had had since she was at school. She was clearly pregnant and I felt a touch of envy of Trevor, who smiled tenderly at her as she gently stroked her bulge. After pressing her cheek against mine and saying hullo to Jacky, she served sherry from a tray, with glasses on doilies.

She seemed like a hostess in a glossy magazine, busy with fussy suburban trifles. I at once felt uneasy at my own condescension and said, "Thanks very much. This gives a nice sense of occasion. Cheers! And what a lovely house!"

Margaret took Jacky into the kitchen, where she could be heard talking excitedly about the thrills and fears of approaching motherhood. They were hitting it off and everything was going as I had hoped. I listened sympathetically to Trevor. "What I really want is a grove of fruit trees and a carpet of turf on the back garden. It's fairly large and just rough earth, but come back in six months' time, Joe, and you'll see a big difference."

"I'm sure I will. You have it very nice here. I'm less keen on gardening than you are. I'd be satisfied with a rambling old townhouse in which I could disappear on my own for a while for a good read. The only trouble would be the constant spending on roof repairs and so on."

Trevor remained silent for half a minute, before replying quietly, "I've got something to talk about in private. Let's go to the pub for a quick one." He called out, "Margaret, I'm just taking Joe for a drink. We won't be long - back in less than half an hour."

"You'd better be. If you're not, the chicken will be over-done and there'll be no sherry left."

I waited apprehensively for a comment from Jacky, who came in, rolled her eyes and frowned, before telling them off: "It's obviously a fait accompli. You men expect us to stay at home like our mothers, but I tell you, it's all going to change, just you wait and see."

I saw that Margaret was uncomfortable with Jacky's belligerence, as I waited while Trevor carefully put on his trilby. She said with a laugh, "He thinks it makes him look like Frankie Sinatra."

It was only a short walk to the male retreat, which had grey, stone walls inside and shiny black tables bolted to the tiled floor. Before me was the familiar scene of men perfectly relaxed, without a woman in sight to cause them to watch what they said or drank.

"It's just a filling station added to the estate, like the newsagent's and the hairdresser's," Trevor said. He insisted on buying the pints, and went through the motions of pointing out some of the men standing at or leaning on the bar, identifying to me a well-known footballer and the plumber who had put in the central heating. At last he paused, and I knew it was confession time.

"It's very nice in the bungalow, Joe, but the loss of Margaret's wages when she gives up her job will make it difficult. We think she should stay at home to look after the child. Our mothers did it, so why shouldn't she? Well, that's her view of the matter. Anyhow, the long and short of it is, I'm thinking of applying for the next Principal Lecturer job."

I knew what Trevor meant. He wanted to give up his job as Union secretary so as to give himself a chance - a very good chance - of becoming a P.L.

I said tartly, "Well, Jones will be so pleased, he will almost certainly reward you."

"What do you think about it?"

I covered up my disappointment. Our partnership was a source of strength for the Union. But I knew what Trevor really wanted. There was only one answer.

"You shouldn't have to make a choice between promotion and the Union, but in reality you have to. You'll never forgive yourself if you throw it away, so have a go."

I saw relief in Trevor's face and in his tone of voice, as with compulsive fluency he said, "There are some good men in Engineering. I think one of them will take over from me and may do a better job. I'm drawn two ways. My father represented his fellow workers for most of his life. He wouldn't have swopped it for the foreman's job. That's what I'll be doing."

"I know your history. But then, when your dad worked on the shop floor, he never thought of buying his own house."

I broke off: "Hell, look who's coming in and waving to us! The young fellow in second lieutenant's uniform must be his son."

"My two favourite suspects!" roared Gerry Jones, advancing towards them, socially at ease, as though his altercations with me had not occurred. "I'm just giving Tim a lift to the railway station. He's due back at his camp tonight. We allowed plenty of time for a few quick ones."

I said provocatively, "I don't suppose you mind that he'll see no action at Suez."

Tim seemed annoyed, as he looked me up and down before saying dismissively, "More's the pity. It's a loss of nerve. The Tories are as guilty as the Socialists. Soft living - that's about all we as a nation seem to be interested in. No wonder so many people are emigrating."

"I'm surprised you don't criticise them for desertion."

Jones interrupted me and turned to Trevor. "What do you think about the challenge to our nation?"

Trevor went pink and said hesitantly that during his army National Service he'd been no further abroad than Essex. "I think we've done what we can in the Middle East."

He avoided my eye as he added, "It had to be done, but we've reached the limit."

Jones grinned. "So," he said dramatically, "you have parted company with Joe over Suez. That is news. There's hope for you yet, Trevor."

Turning to his son, he added, "Never mind what Joe says, he's always the odd man out. He'll have to watch his step, as I've already advised him, but now's not the time to talk about it. I'll get our beers and a whisky for everyone."

Three-quarters of an hour later, after a couple more drinks, I walked hurriedly behind my friend out of the pub. Trevor looked hangdog and spoke with agitation: "The point is, it's all over now. There was no harm done in pulling some wool over Jones's eyes."

"The trouble is, once you back-pedal in your dealings with a persuasive character like that, you'll find it hard not to carry on doing it, on one issue after another."

I realised I had spoken sharply, as Trevor raced ahead of me, without replying. We continued in silence back to the bungalow, where we tiptoed like Helen Shapiro along the hallway to the living room.

Margaret came out of the kitchen, aglow, with her bulge newly draped in a grey, sleeveless dress. She was not out of sorts with us but said in a shrill tone, "You took your time! I only had a glass and a half of sherry, because of the baby, but Jacky finished the bottle."

Turning to me, she added, "Who's looking at me, kid? Not bad development for four months, is it?"

"I couldn't do better myself. By the way, when you and Jacky are talking, the melodies of the different Welsh tones combine very well. I think they call it counterpoint."

"That's a posh word. I've only ever heard it at the Eisteddfod."

Jacky skipped into the room, her face flushed by the sherry, and said sonorously, "Is that the smooth-talking union man, trying a bit of flattery to take our eyes off the clock?"

Margaret replied calmly, "Well, we had quite a nice time while they were out of the way. And Joe's quite right about the accents. Of course, we're real Wales in Prestatyn, where I come from. We still have the Celtic traditions, as well as some gold in our hills. My uncle dug some out for a ring for the Queen, when she was married."

As I expected, Jacky could not let that pass. "Ho ho ho! O boyo! A few bits of gold for royalty! Get away with you! Give me coal and Nye Bevan, any day."

Margaret became more spirited. "What's wrong with royalty then? They set a very good example of family life. The Coronation was very popular and we enjoyed ourselves, didn't we, Trevor?"

Trevor shot me another guilty look before conceding that they had had a good time.

Jacky laughed and exclaimed, "It's all a pantomime! The Kings and Queens of England have never been interested in Wales."

Margaret pursed her lips and said in a dismissive voice, "That's not true. I remember when I was a small child, the King visited South Wales and said that something should be done about the unemployment."

"Yes, three weeks later he abdicated and hasn't set foot there since. Over the centuries they built castles on the borders to dominate us. "

"Maybe, but look at all the Welsh people who have made good in England."

Her eyes running with tears of mirth, Jacky put one arm round my shoulder and the other round Trevor's and tried to dance the Palais glide, until Margaret came right up to her and wagging her finger said very loudly, "There's nothing wrong with Ivor Novella, but I was thinking of all those who have got to the top in the Government. Even your friend Bevan did a good job with the NHS. I can't complain about my care in recent months, and I'm going to the local hospital to have the baby."

I recognised her conciliatory tone and invitation to change the subject, but Jacky would not let go. "Men of ambition," she started, slurring the last syllable. "Men of ambi-shun will always go where the power lies."

"Atten-shun!" shouted Trevor, apparently desperate to lighten the atmosphere. "By the left, quick march!"

The two of us set off in step into the kitchen and back into the. Lounge, da-da-da-ing the *RAF March Past*, until Margaret shouted, "Don't you want any dinner, today?"

Jacky piped up from her armchair, "Just you tell the selfish oafs!"

Trevor set about opening a bottle of Chianti, talking loudly to me about nothing much. Then we all
sat at the table, Margaret brought in the tomato soup, and quietness ruled, until I said, "This is lovely, Margaret. You are a wife-and-a -half. Let's have a toast to you and your family to be!"

Jacky then said, "Sorry if I was a bit boisterous. It's just that one day, I'm sure, Wales will have its own Government, so that we can have more self-respect."

Don't insist on the last word or you'll start it up again," replied Margaret, testily. "I have plenty of self - respect, and so have you!"

Jacky entered a subdued and patient lecturing mode. "I'm sure you have. But how do you feel when someone is accused of Welshing? A conquered people always have to suffer prejudice."

"Yes, I know, but we don't have to harp on about it all the time. We should be proud of our beautiful country, not only in my part of Wales, especially Snowdonia, but down on the Gower peninsular, which you must know really well."

Jacky persisted as Joe knew she would: "Wales to me is first and foremost the Gwent and Glamorgan valleys, where children and women in filthy rags worked underground or sweated in dangerous jobs in the iron foundries, making profits for their bosses living in mansions, many of them in London."

"I know a bit about that, Jacky." Margaret's fire was not spent. "I remember learning in school about the Maids of Rebecca, setting the toll-houses on fire."

"And also about the Chartist movement?"

"Yes, but that was English. It wasn't a Welsh thing."

"Oh yes it was. It wasn't the English who took up arms against the soldiers of Queen Victoria. But the Welsh did, at Newport. The valleys were ringed with military bases. We were under siege."

"Okay. That's all history. Nowadays, wages are high and there are far more opportunities. Look at you – you aren't pulling a load along a tramway, you've got a very good job."

It was after three and we were all hungry. The chicken was not too dry and all except Margaret washed it down with more Italian red, which I hoped would make Jacky drowsy, until she suddenly exclaimed, "I know that times have changed but Wales is still ruled by England."

"Oh, shut up!" Margaret lashed out. "We don't seem to agree on anything. Trevor told me to expect both you and Joe to be worked up about our invasion of Egypt. I tell you, I held my head high when we went into action against that tinpot dictator. And most people agree with me - or don't think about it at all. Britain doesn't really change, you know.

"Anyway, Britain had most of the shares in the company owning the Canal. What about international law? It surely doesn't allow the Egyptians to confiscate our assets. I tell you, the only reason the Americans forced us out was to get in with the Egyptian themselves. They want to be top dogs and to hell with the British Empire."

I butted in: "You're right, Margaret, that the question of the legality of Nasser's action has been debated. But in general it's accepted that he was in the right as he was only acting inside his own country. Anyhow, as we have pulled out, there's not much more to be said, is there? There's no point in us falling out over it."

"Oh yes, there is!" Jacky shouted. "If the poor and homeless in Egypt heard you talk, they'd think you were sitting pretty behind your picture window, with no concern for them. You make me squirm with embarrass...embarrassment."

She slumped over the table, humming *Land Of My Fathers*, while Trevor, white with silent rage, glared at her. Tears ran down Margaret's cheeks and she said she felt tired and had to lie down.

I had intended before Jacky's climactic outburst to propose a mock motion that they finished their dinner without further dissension, but saw it was too late to mend the damage. "We'd better go now,"

I said. "Thanks for a very nice meal – and for your company."

I seized Jacky by the arm and led her out to the hall and grimaced resignedly at Trevor, who nearly spoiled the day. Upsetting Margaret like that when she was pregnant wasn't funny."

"Sorry, Joe. The sherry and the wine went to my head. I'll write and apologise to her."

I was pacified by her contrite tone, and back home followed her into the bedroom, where she removed her blue woollen skirt and stood smiling as she undid her suspender belt, pulled off a stocking and waved it in the air. I was not at ease as I undressed, but she moved on top of me and made a few strong movements that elicited no physical response. She sat up and said in a lachrymose tone, "Oh boy, so you don't feel turned on. What a shame, especially as your bed is so nice and bouncy. Never mind, can I have something to eat? I didn't eat much of Margaret's dinner.

I made a cheese salad and took it into the bedroom, but Jacky was asleep, snoring slightly. I shook my head. Equality of the sexes was one thing, but I was beginning to feel like a fly clambering over a spider's web. My feet felt very sticky. I could see we had a lot in common politically but I doubted if it was enough for a good relationship. I'd never get used to her brash manner.

I returned to my living room and tuned listlessly into a play on the Home Service, but gave up after five minutes and started my game of going through my mind's table of failed relationships. When I was in bed I decided it had been a mediocre Boxing Day, without even taking account of Trevor's decision to leave the fold. Jones's comment that I should watch my step came to mind but was soon driven out by sleep.

CHAPTER NINE

The Spring term had only just started but limped along as dull as the sky and the grimy piles of snow in the streets. My students seemed remote and impersonal and when they were making notes as I talked about Keynes, the gloomy thought came to me that I was like the slot machine from which they took their cigarettes. Another fencing match with the Principal could not come too soon. The past seemed a prison from which I could not escape. You are a damn fool, pandering to your nostalgia by sending a Christmas card to Jenny, care of the hospital, with a good-wishes message, signed Joe Bachelor. Really, you want to sleep with her. She'll understand.

A day later, all traces of despondency were dispersed by wild optimism, when the postman brought a letter with a Salop post imprint. I knew at once who had sent it. The only person who could have given her my address was Polly. It turned out I was right on both counts. There was no hesitation or pretence in Jenny's message; she said plainly, "I'm divorced. Let's meet for a drink for the sake of old times, seven years after we met on the train."

I laughed loud with delight at the phrase "old times," since our romance had lasted only an hour, though every detail came back to me, as I drove on the following Saturday to the meeting place outside the town hall in Shrewsbury. I didn't care if she had put on as much weight as I had. In fact, she looked only slightly heavier and her face was barely creased. Her waist was still fairly slim, unlike mine.

"Where did you get that paunch?" was the first thing she said. "Are you sure you are the man I met on the train? Now, don't blush, it doesn't matter."

"I need to take more exercise, I go everywhere by car. Perhaps I should have a job walking the wards."

"Like me. I'm a ward sister, at the same hospital. I shall probably stay there forever, as I like it."

"Give me a potted history of yourself in the years since that time on the train."

"Well, I was very disappointed in you, for months after we first met. You seemed to be yet another superficial smart Alec, like most of the young doctors I met, who thought they were gods for women to worship. They picked you up and dropped you when they had had enough. But I didn't learn. I married a doctor who had been very persistent in his attentions.

"Eventually, he decided his future lay in Australia as a consultant, and assumed I would go along. I had no desire to follow him, but it was not as easy a decision as it sounds, the way I'm putting it. I prize my independence, but divorce is not an easy step to take, especially for a woman. Even my mother supported tradition and said I should go with him. And then I remembered our conversation on the train, and the social and political affinity between us, and I knew I wanted to meet someone just like you, and when your card arrived, I thought, why not you?

"Well, thanks for the speech. You've said it all, and I feel the same about you. I had better tell you, I was married too, only for a couple of years."

"Tell me everything, you dark horse! Come on, let's have a cup of coffee. I want to know all the grisly details."

So I told her about Julie. She said, "In short, your marriage did not last, any longer than mine did. It's something else we have in common. All right then. Where were we, before that little diversion?"

She grinned, and her warmth flowed into me. I hugged her quickly, and thought we could really start again, and see how we got on. I held her hand, as we walked through the streets, engaging in subjects of polite conversation. I could hardly believe it, as we carried on in the same vein of easy talk, where we left off in the train.

"I'm glad you're not wearing a little hat with veil and feathers."

"What do you take me for? A home and garden woman, exchanging cake recipes with the neighbours?"

"No. You have a job outside the home, like most women in wartime. You're equal to men."

"At least. I'm a member of a women's group. We organised a march locally protesting against the Miss World contest. "

As we began to exchange ideas, I felt I was the more stilted talker. "There's a lot of political apathy, today," I said. "John Osborne's dead right about that. I went up to see *Look back in Anger*, in the summer.

104

My parents and your mother had the Spanish Civil War to be passionate about. Today, people seem to feel very little excitement about anything, except Bill Haley. They seemed about evenly divided on support for Eden over Suez."

"Well, I quite like *Rock Around the Clock*, but I was always been opposed to war with Egypt. I thought Gaitskell was very gung ho at the beginning of August, and Nye Bevan wasn't much better".

"Yes, fortunately, they changed their tune, though it wasn't so important, as the Yanks pulled the rug from under Eden. They'll have their own agenda for the Middle East. They won't be sorry to take the old colonial power down a peg or two."

"Or they may not want to give Russia an excuse to get more involved there."

"Well, I'd like to see people stirred up politically, but it won't be an easy number."

"You're probably right. Most kids are just happy in their hula-hoops or listening to a jukebox. Still, I have to admire some of the young nurses who have their own skiffle group."

"I bet thcy look good, with their sweater-girl bras and fluorescent socks."

"I'm sure they'd be of interest to you. Give me Marlon Brando, any time."

"Well, I like him too."

"By the way, is Granddad still around?"

"I'm afraid he died, three years ago. I often think of him. Despite his vanity, which had its appeal for me as a teenager, he helped to lift my spirits after dad died,"

I felt happy as we went with the flow of everyday

conversation and was also pleased that we agreed with the fading message whitewashed on a wall, *No To German Rearmament.*

"That's a good slogan," I said, "but I'm not entirely sure where I stand politically."

"I'm much the same, though I'm sure we share the same socialist principles."

Her face was glowing with high spirits. "There was something I always intended to tell you, one fine day," she said impetuously, or perhaps you guessed. It was not just chance that brought us together on that train. You may have thought it unusual when I came in and sat down opposite you. The fact is, I saw you getting on and thought how fine you looked in your Air Force blue. I wouldn't normally have entered a compartment with a strange man, but I made an exception. You looked warm and compassionate."

"I liked being picked up, and really wanted you. I made the biggest mistake of my life, when I let you go."

"Maybe. But what now?"

"How about next week-end at the sea-side?"

"A dirty week-end? All right," she said. "But I'm working Saturday. Could you make it Sunday, picking me up at my mother's place in Coventry, where she still lives? I've got three days off."

"Okay, and then we'll be off down the Fosse. Come back early on Tuesday morning. My classes on Monday are taken by my friend Trevor, later in the week, and so we'll swop days - we've done it before."

106

We set off for Bournemouth early on the Sunday, making good time in the teeth of showers and rough winds. I took a hand from the steering wheel and put it on her shoulder, touching her hair, which was now blonde-streaked and had a fresh, scented smell. I said jauntily, "Very good going - less than two hours till we're there."

Jenny leaned across the long gear lever and gave me a squeeze round the waist. She replied as dryly as he had expected: "That's not bad for a pre-war baby Morris. Shame the Russians can't go as fast out of Hungary."

I ignored her challenge to a political argument and pulled up on a grass verge next to an arable field blacker than the storm clouds. At the far side, a herd of cows formed a line behind a low hedge and peered across at the little black car.

"Poor things!" she had cried, as she took out their sandwiches. They're like women queuing at a public convenience."

"I thought you were going to wind me up. I expected you to say they were standing still, like the Soviet tanks."

"Quite right. I should have said that. Now you've reminded me, I think I'll try to get the news."

She fiddled for ages with her portable radio until we heard through the interference a rhythmic crowd noise, which the reporter in Budapest interpreted as "Russians go home!"

I shrugged my shoulders. "They are leaving, anyhow." I didn't want to pursue it any further. She had opinions at least as strong as mine. I knew I mustn't fall out with her, or the weekend could end in disaster. She had brought along a wedding ring. "It's not from my marriage. It's one I played with as a child. I'm not as unconventional as you think. It'll save embarrassment and besides, the landlady will probably be like my mother."

I met Veronica, her mother, before we set off. She had a council flat just off the Coventry by-pass, near the Standard car factory. Speaking in a quiet, hesitant tone, she was apologetic about the linoleum. "I'm saving up for a wall to wall carpet and my first Hoover. Things are getting better, aren't they?"

"Well, from what I've heard, you did your bit to help improve society. Don't you think we could do with more socialism – youth clubs and higher pensions, for example, instead of atom bombs?"

"I agree, but it's up to the young ones to fight for it. When I look into the mirror, I see a lined, weary face. I must admit I've lost most of my enthusiasm for the causes that once inspired me."

She livened up on the subject of Bournemouth, saying she thought it strange that we were going away in November. "I suppose you will be staying" - she searched for the word – "separately." We agreed with her, without any intention of doing so.

"It's silly and expensive, and very pre-war," said Jenny, when we were alone.

"Yes, you wouldn't think someone who once supported social revolution would have such old-fashioned values. Anyhow, we are both fairly experienced, as she knows."

"Don't be smug. I can understand her worries. She was unmarried when she had me. It's a price she doesn't want me to pay."

Advance booking had seemed unnecessary, as it was out of season. We drove close to the sea front and stopped at a large, semi-detached Edwardian house displaying a vacancies sign on a post, near a flagpole with a bedraggled Union Jack. A lank, middle-aged woman who was taking shirts off the line was faintly embarrassed:

"Sorry about the washing. I didn't expect any visitors. We don't normally get anyone this late. Pleased to meet you. I'm Doris," she added, with a conspicuous glance at Jenny's ring. "Come and meet my husband, Alf."

Alf was about fifty-five, with bulging eyes that roved over the visitors and lingered on their separate suitcases. He wore a faded army sweater and insisted that he carry Jenny's case inside and that they have a drink in a dreary private sitting room, with an Axminster fitted carpet.

Alf said he had been a warrant officer in the war. "I was in Signals. I got to know the wogs in Egypt. I wasn't surprised they tried to steal the Canal. Still, the Jews taught them a lesson. They aren't my favourite people but I cheered when they went into Sinai. One day we'll finish Nasser off."

I said stiffly, "I don't think so. They have the right to nationalise the canal, and the American wouldn't let us get away with it."

"It don't matter about the Yanks. You'll see - the time will come when we bomb Cairo."

There was silence until I stood up and excused Jenny and myself. "You know, I said, when we reached our room, "the Israeli attack was only about a week after the Tory conference, when Eden threatened to use force to take the Canal. It's too much of a coincidence. They must have planned it together - and probably with France."

"Yes, Israel started it, so that we could finish it."

"Eden made a huge gamble, and lost it."

A few minutes later, we were lying on the bed, holding each other cautiously, as though guarding against breakages, when Jenny said, "We can have sex, but not without safeguards."

"Of course. I know all about them. They're in my wallet."

"They aren't enough. They have been known to break."

We got, up and went for a cold walk by the sea, past boarded up huts where bird droppings and remnants of the holiday season's litter rotted out of reach of the waves thrashing the shore. I went to the chemist's in the town, wondering why we had not talked openly about contraception before we came away together. I cursed inwardly at the thought that although I had been married I was nearly as shy about sex as my parents had been. With a rush of emotional liberation from convention, I composed my features into a mask of assurance and loudly asked the lady assistant for the gels in a jar that Jenny had recommended.

We went back to the guesthouse, expecting time for experiments before dinner but I made a flip remark that I at once regretted. "What price the

Hungarian revolution now? Suez has taken the heat off the Russians and in fact they don't sound so guilty now, do they?"

She cried out as though he had hit her. "Joe, the Hungarian revolution isn't about having fitted refrigerators and nylon shirts. It's about having an opposition and a free press."

"Perhaps it is. I see the force of what you say. It's just that I can also understand why the Russians after two invasions from the west in a generation, are dead against the risk of a capitalist state and even an American base on their border. On the other hand, I think they are exaggerating their vulnerability to attack. Their thinking is too rigid. It isn't like June 1941. They've had atomic weapons themselves for the last seven years. That's their ultimate deterrent to potential aggression."

We agreed that the gap between our viewpoints was not a chasm and started to caress each other, but the bell rang for us to go down to the silent dining room, where we toyed with the wooden rings around our table napkins and cast glances at the sea landscapes hung against the maroon flock wallpaper. We relaxed when Al brought in the lamb roast, but his manner with us was short and when he came in with the custard and tart, he nervously cleared his throat and said agitatedly, "I went into your room to turn the bedclothes down, though I guessed it was probably unnecessary. I help Doris with most jobs in the guesthouse. I couldn't help noticing your pickled onions in a jar. Very small ones they were. Did you buy them in Bournemouth?"

He had barely asked his question when Jenny's angry reply drew the wind from his sails: "Have you got a funny sense of humour or don't you know what they are? They're pessaries to stop me becoming pregnant!"

Alf winced at the words and scuttled out of the room, returning a minute or two later with Doris, who was full of wrath:

"How dare you use words like that to my husband! It was not right to leave those things out on the table in your room. You aren't even married. You're watching each other all the time to see if you're playing the part."

I cut in: "What's it got to do with you? Who do you think you are - Queen Victoria and Prince Albert? It's nearly 1960, for Christ's sake!"

Alf found some more courage: "We don't like your language - birth control and all that. It takes me back to my time in the service. You don't talk about it in mixed company. Please leave, first thing in the morning. You can stay the night, as it's late. We only want married couples in our house. Find a place where they're less particular about who they take in."

Jenny said vehemently, "No, thank you! We come here to relax, and we get criticised by narrow-minded people who should be in a museum. We'll leave you to play war games with Anthony Eden."

She stormed upstairs and started to pack her luggage. I followed her, after exchanging ritual glares with Alf. I held her close until she relaxed and gave me a long kiss. "Let's go home," she said. "I forgot to tell you. Mother decided to stay with Aunt

Alice, her sister, as I was going away. We shall be on our own."

We paid for our dinner in sullen silence and drove to the front, where the waves were breaking against the promenade. I stroked her hair and face, wishing there was room enough on the back seat to suggest making love, but glad that our arguments had been blown away by the storm in the guesthouse. It was after midnight when we set off through the shadows and pools of yellow lamplight in deserted suburbia and it was just starting to get light when we reached Jenny's home. We parked round the corner, out of sight of the neighbours, and tiptoed up the path.

Jenny went into the kitchen to make a cup of tea, while I tinkered with her radio. There was no interference so early in the morning, but I could find nothing on the World Service.

She spoke briskly from the doorway: "Never mind Hungary for the time being. We'll just have to go on living with our differences. Time will come when you will probably think more like I do. It'll need patience. You're open about your beliefs and when I think of people like Alf, I want to take you in my arms. Let's go to bed. I'll get the pickled onions out of my bag."

She took off her white sweater and her skirt, and he smiled when he saw her blue girdle. "You may not have been in the Forces, but you're well disciplined."

"It subdues a few of my bulges, so you don't notice them, when I'm dressed up."

We exchanged soft kisses in the grey light and I caressed her tentatively but when she hugged me I

113

pressed my body over hers and wrapped her in my legs. I went inside her quickly and we cried out together. As we lay holding hands over the damp patch left on the sheet by the onions, I thought aloud how well it had gone, as though we had practised together for a long time.

Jenny's comment was earthier: "I think we were both full of lust, don't you? They say it's a good basis for marriage, so watch out. I'll be after you." My smile grew and she laughed as her free hand traced a line down my body to my hairs. As she lowered herself onto me, I grinned and said, "Your damsons are ripe enough to be picked."

"They're my daggers to press into you, like you enter me. Now!"

We dozed and touched each other until mid-morning.

"Cup of tea?" she asked.

"On one condition. You must leap out of bed without any clothes on. Not like in the films when the girl always pulls a sheet over her."

"All right."

She did as I asked and the swing of her low, pointed breasts on the stocky figure with the narrow waist was just as I had imagined on the train.

Later on, I wandered round the living room, looking at photographs of Jenny as a child and of her mother as a young woman, without the lines.

"Has Veronica never said what your dad was like?"

"Not really. I don't think she has ever wanted me to know much about him, in case I got too curious. She has never wanted anything to do with him. I think in the old days, crowds of people came together in demonstrations and meetings, bound by a camaraderie that didn't necessarily lead to close friendships. She had an impulsive relationship but it didn't mean she ever wanted to hang on to my father. I suppose you could say he served the purpose of the moment and also gave her a present for the long term. I believe she has always been glad to have me."

"Wouldn't you like to know who he was - or is?"

"Yes and no. I would never do anything to upset mother. I do know I got my fair hair from him and she once called him Edward. He came from somewhere by Cadbury's village, in Birmingham, and she met him at a meeting. To save him from waiting on the station platform for the milk train, she offered to put him up for the night, and that was that."

I let her words sink in. It couldn't be true. But I knew it was. The world of the comrades had been a small one. Ted was a fairly common name but Edward was rarely one spoken by manual workers. His father's hair had been fair, and he lived near the Bourneville village. He had often spoken at meetings in Coventry, and he had stayed overnight in comrades' homes. It was the custom. They didn't have cars to get them home late. I turned to Jenny, who was staring at me, as though she apprehended what I was about to say:

"I may be your half-brother."

"Your father was Edward?" she screamed. "You know what we've done? It's called incest."

We clung together but did not kiss. I felt her heart beating like a bell being tolled with furious energy. I told her all about Edward. Then we sat listlessly, saying nothing.

"We are only half-related," I said. "Anyway, it's not certain; Edward's a fairly common name."

She shook her head, as she wept "It's as good as a certainty that there wasn't another Communist called Edward who used to travel around the Birmingham area speaking at meetings. You ask if it matters. Of course it does! Can you think of anything worse we could have done? I can't. I want children. Would you seriously risk becoming the father to your sister's - or half-sister's child? Thank goodness there was not much chance of that. You realise it would have meant an illegal abortion?"

"I don't want to think about it. Can we still see each, one day, other as friends?"

"I don't know. Why are you so bloody phlegmatic? Don't you realise we've broken the biggest social taboo of all? We'd be outcasts if it ever got out. Thank goodness we had double contraception."

"Maybe I am a buttoned -up person - until I suddenly let go. But we have a saving grace. We didn't know in advance anything about a blood relationship. Maybe sometime, a friendship will be possible."

"Perhaps, one day. But don't delude yourself. You know what would happen if we carried on meeting now."

Jenny was crying inconsolably when I left her. She pushed me away from her and I went home almost in a trance, knowing what had happened but still not reacting fully to it emotionally. I slumped into my armchair, and then my own tears started, as loneliness and despair cut into me. I knew I loved Jenny with the truest feeling I could ever have. I jumped up from the chair and paced the room, unable to concentrate on anything except my own misery.

I glanced at the painted ladies on the wall, wishing they would smile in sympathy, but they cast cool glances at me from under lowered eyelids. I opened the Dansette and put on Beethoven's Pastoral, but it did not cheer me up.

I was awake that night, vainly trying various sleep positions, while images of Jenny insistently played on my mind. I slept for about an hour until it was time to get up. I drove vacantly to College and spent a blurry day.

I had to have it out with mother. That evening, I drove vengefully across town to the old family home in Selly Oak. She looked at me with fearful features, and almost curled into a ball, as my reproaches pierced her. Then she had confirmed what Jenny and I had three-parts believed.

"Oh, Joe, I am so sorry. It should never have happened. Edward was a bit like his father."

"It really gets to me. I remember you and Edward arguing with Aunt Mary, the day war broke out. You said, 'Some of us always tell the truth.' But you kept quiet about my half-sister."

"We didn't want any reminders. I told him, and he agreed he must never see the other woman again, and I'm sure he didn't, although his agreement not to see his child was a big price to pay. We carried on

117

our life together as though it had never happened. I think Grandma knew about it."

Her stoicism was easy to imagine, but not her submerged feelings, which rarely came to the surface. I had wanted to tear away her defences with fierce criticism, but instead started to work it off in the garden of the old family council house, cutting back the elderberry bushes that threw a shade over the kitchen window. When I went inside again, she surprised me by clasping my hand and looking at me fondly, loosening the rein on her emotions as she had done on the eve of my wedding, when she had asked me with anguish if I thought that Julie really loved me. I told her that Jenny was just someone I had met and she asked no questions. It was the tight-lipped behaviour trait that I disliked but knew we shared.

She had been embarrassed recently by a jocular remark on the radio about a woman wanting her boyfriend's body. At university I had quickly shed many restraints and later on married Julie but still found it difficult to talk to mother about relationships or even to show her how much I cared for her.

CHAPTER 10

A fortnight later, I stumbled yawning from the bedroom to the kitchen, which didn't seem quite in order, what with the kettle next to the cooker instead of by the sink, and the cups and plates and cutlery all in a heap, as though they had been moved to allow someone to step onto the worktop without making a noise.

Perhaps someone had put an arm through the gap made by the small, hinged window, in order to open the large window. It must have been a thief, or a homeless person looking for somewhere to bed down, or an undercover agent. I pulled myself together. Nothing seemed to be missing. The intruder was imaginary. I'd had the rows in London but it was the awful parting from Jenny that agitated me when I sat alone in my apartment. I'd tried to blot it all out with a few drinks.

Still, who was to say? I might have a new student in class, wearing a raincoat and carrying a rolled umbrella. Or it might be a tall blonde, skilled in seduction. "Yes, Caroline," I could say, "I learned the Morse code when I was doing my national service. In the early hours I tapped out secrets for Nasser, like how many Walls sausages the British soldier has for breakfast. I have more to tell you. Where shall we go this evening?"

Fingal's Cave was playing really loud as I ate my cornflakes listlessly. It was freezing cold in my car, and I urged on the whining starter motor: "Come on, please, Morris."

Glancing up, as a shadow fell on the dashboard, I saw the postman, and lowering the window called out, "Hallo there, Mohinder! The air's like ice. You'd be better off in the foundry."

"I wouldn't work there again. I like fresh air. Besides, I'm trying to use my M.A. in Mathematics by becoming a teacher."

"I hope you make it. There's nothing wrong with your English."

"I hope not. I grew up with English people in the Punjab."

"I'll write a reference if it'll help you. Ring me at the college, or I tell you what, are you free Saturday lunchtime? You are? Right, I'll meet you in the Weaver's Arms at about one o'clock and you can tell me exactly what you want. Just at the moment, I'm going nowhere."

"I'll give you a hand, Joe. And I've got a letter for you."

I felt bad about the panting figure pushing me for fifteen yards along the road. My heart beat fast when I looked at the envelope and saw Jenny's handwriting. I left it lying on the passenger seat during the drive to the college, so that I could speculate what was inside, and perhaps postpone seeing a message I didn't want to hear. She may be saying she misses me, but it could be that she's marrying a doctor, or has changed her mind and is about to emigrate to Australia.

On the way in to work I amused myself by giving searching looks to cars parked by the roadside, as I recalled cheap films in which detectives in stationary cars started their engines and closely tailed the suspect, who never became aware of what was happening, even when there were no other cars on the street.

I tore open the envelope as soon as I had parked, and was only slightly deflated to read a circular letter, signed by Jenny as secretary, publicising a group calling for the Government to stop the nuclear weapons programme. They were sure their movement would grow. I fancied I could see her soft but challenging features, and speculated on getting to Shropshire and back and still having enough of my month's petrol ration left for us to drive around together. I knew it was just daydreaming. Private encounters were not going to happen.

But the message she had sent me was still sinking in, as I entered the college's Victorian building, its oak floor scarred by the passage of many thousands of students, some of them remembered on boards *For the Fallen*, on the wall in the corridor. I imagined men with moustaches and wearing hats with brims, jostling on the staircases alongside girls with wide crinoline skirts and long hair. Some of the men would have died in South Africa and many more a few years later in France. The girls were the widows in waiting. Two more decades produced the Second World War, but the college had given up recording names, perhaps because it would have looked too much like a regular pattern, which was an uncomfortable idea. And now most people seemed to shrug off the nuclear threat.

I ran my hand along the solid balustrade, as I went up a floor to the General Studies staff room, where Trevor was seated, already busy with the paperwork that went with his recent promotion. I J a lecturer."

I wondered if my friend had rehearsed his words in conversation with Jones, over a whisky. I had replied mildly, "A reprimand is good enough, Trev. He's a good teacher, well-liked by the students, the men as well as the women."

Trevor had congratulated me tersely, after I succeeded in persuading the Governing Body to keep the young man on, much to Jones' annoyance, which showed under his aggressive bonhomie.

Trevor's responded sharply, when I mentioned that I had had a letter from a girl who was campaigning to ban the bomb. "It's surrender. The real issue is whether we are to stay an important power. If we are to be taken seriously throughout the world, we have to stay strong. Our standard of living depends on it."

"Oh, come off it, Trev, that's the Suez argument all over again. You're saying Britain has another chance to rule the world, now we've got a new status symbol. All it means is that we can spread Strontium 90 over an island in the Pacific – some barbaric place, lacking our civilization."

"Well, you go off to demonstrate in Trafalgar Square again, Joe, as much as you like. You won't change anything, because most people don't trust the Russians, even though you think theirs is the Promised Land."

"No, I don't. It'll take time before they have it good materially, and anyone can say anything they like. They'll get there, if they're not bankrupted by armaments."

"Well, why can't they disarm?"

"Neither Russia nor America dare to do it, as they are afraid of each other. But we could do it."

"I suggested, not long ago, that you go to Russia, to see for yourself. You might find a nice girl – you know a Natasha or an Olga."

"Actually, that isn't a bad idea. Anyway, come for a game of darts in the Weavers tonight, and we'll sort out all life's problems."

The following morning was Saturday and I was in no hurry to get up, until I heard the rap of the letterbox lid. I took the only letter back to bed, and read without emotion:

"Dear Joe, This isn't a summons or a bill – I'm typing it at work, in between letters on street closures and car parks. I am writing on impulse, but I think it expresses how I really feel, when I say it's time we thought of our future together. You're a good man, but a bit complicated. You keep your emotions covered. Please let them out. Telephone me at once. Jacky."

I was alarmed that she was coming on so strongly. I knew I did not want a permanent relationship. We shared many political beliefs but that was not enough. I should have had it out with her the morning after the evening at Trevor's but she had left abruptly after breakfast to go to her brother's family in Swansea.

She was in when I rang. "Joe," she said sweetly, "how nice of you to ring, so soon after my letter. I was just thinking of you. How are you?"

"All right. I'm off to the Weavers shortly, just for a pint before paying a visit to mother."

"Sounds nice. I wish I was there with you."

"It's not that attractive. It's a thirties pub, built on the scale of the factories where most of its customers worked."

I hesitated and said solemnly, "I wanted to say something about your letter." There was silence from her. "You can't pressurise me to stay with you. It's the end of the line for us."

"You cold bastard!"

She banged the phone down, to my great relief. In high spirits I dialled the operator and asked for the Shropshire number on Jenny's letter. I had expected it to be her private line, but was quickly connected to her ward at the hospital. I asked to speak to nurse Jenny After a tense wait, I heard her say, "Hallo, Joe, I'm at the same place, but I'm a sister now."

"I'm not surprised – after all, you were already half a one, to me."

"I should tell you to get lost, though nurses usually use stronger expressions. What would you say to that?"

"That would be a very un-sisterly rejection. I have a better idea. Why not let me come with you to your next anti-nuclear public outing?"

"Good God, Joe! How can you suggest that we go out together? I was torn apart by what happened between us. My impression was that you were too."

"I was, and I am. It's just that real friendship is rare. I don't want to waste it."

"Very well. I'll introduce you to a friend. He works at my hospital. There's a women's demonstration in London on Sunday week. We shall be in the Square at three o'clock, wearing black sashes. You can watch."

"Are you very good friends?"

"Not as good as you and I once were."

"In that case, I'll come."

I did not want the conversation to stop. "So you're a sister in Salop. I love Shropshire – definitely one of my favourite counties. It's all contrasts - red, black and chocolate coloured soils, and there's the hills, not so wild as those in Wales."

"That's enough, you literary show-off, but, it is very nice here."

There was silence, before her words rushed out as though she had rehearsed them: "It's no good, Joe. It can't be as it was between us. Anyway, you'll certainly have someone by now."

"I did have but it's over."

"You soon found consolation when we parted. If I thought you were just a cheap philanderer, I wouldn't want to set eyes on you again."

"I made a mistake," I said humbly, but was gratified by the emotion that had entered her tone. I told her something of Jacky's hectoring style. "I have not stopped thinking of you."

"All right, then. A neurotic girlfriend had you cornered. It's well known in medicine. It's a manipulative technique. You shouldn't have rushed the encounter."

"Well, perhaps a few of us will have a cup of tea after the rally."

"O.K. There's no reason why you shouldn't campaign against nuclear weapons. I only wish the things that concern us worried more people."

"In the Weavers, yesterday, I was talking to a group of students, mostly Indian. They there, in their business suits, debating the merits of the Ford Zephyr against the Sunbeam Talbot, well within their reach when they qualify, next summer.

"I mentioned to them that the number of ships using the canal is getting back to normal. One of them said it was all a storm in a teacup, so long as the nation was getting better off. He said Anthony Eden would soon be forgotten, and I guess he's right. Memories are short when people feel comfortable. There are lots of jobs and new objects of desire, especially cars."

"Hurrah for good times ahead. The petrol ration's going up again. I must go now. Cheerio."

"Auf wiedersehen."

My spirits slightly lifted by the conversation, I set off for the Co-op feeling like a happy tourist visiting an old-fashioned country observing middle-aged assistants, male and female, tying up brown-papered parcels of groceries with string.

I hadn't had time to tell Jenny that I had been in the pub for some time, until Mohinder the postman came in, staying for ten minutes, while we chatted about his job reference. A group of Indians drinking were students at the College. I talked with them about Suez, and the oil business, where two of them, Teja and Joginder, had good jobs ready for them when they qualified in the summer.

I had noticed that Teja was showing some effects of the drink, with his ultra-correct manners slipping into the informal style of "No, Joe," instead of "No, Sir." As the Indian emitted squeals of laughter, he pulled his long locks of hair down over his eyes, and turned to me:

"Did you know I come from a line of nabobs? Let me show you how we dance in the Punjab."

"No, no – if you want to dance, go to the Palais tonight. You'll find lots of gorgeous girls."

Joginder called out, "We are only having a joke. Go on, I dare you, Sir."

Eventually, after several embarrassing refusals with a background of laughter from the students, I gave way to an invitation to dance a slow foxtrot. Pirouetting with exaggerated formality, I made sure that we were never in bodily contact and soon brought the burlesque to an end, but felt uneasy the landlord's shout across the room, "Now then! Let's keep it proper, if you don't mind!"

I walked up to the bar and stared back at the glaring eyes above the moustache of Ugly Bill. I replied brusquely, "Mind what you are saying. There's nothing improper going on, and you know it."

"All I know is, I want you out of my pub – now!"

I turned on my heels and saw in the corner the grinning face of the man I had clashed with over Suez, at the dance. I beat a retreat from the

Weavers, knowing that Malcolm would tell all the college about it.

"Damn, damn, damn!" I said out loud. "I shouldn't have more than two pints at lunch-time. I'd better go home to my record player and find some consolation in Igor's Lament."

CHAPTER 11

I spent the next evening with mother, talking about old times. I could not sustain the anger against her that I had felt. At half-past six the following morning, I dressed quietly and went down to the kitchen, treading on the ends of each stair to avoid the creaking in the middle, as I had done when I was a boy. It would do her good to go back to bed when she found I had gone. It was very cold, and the medieval, black cooker, which she had refused to let me replace, as usual smelled faintly of gas.

I was home before seven and after a leisurely breakfast set out early for College, where I found it hard to settle down to work in the library. I sat doodling and imagining living with Jenny, but perhaps never having children, because of the taboo. I looked through dusty encyclopaedias dating from the nineteen-twenties. There was very little about incest, indeed it seemed a barely mentionable subject. It involved fathers and daughters mainly, and increased the risk of birth of defective children. Also, it undermined the family, as seemed obvious, and I wondered if it was the main reason why it was prohibited. Jenny would know all about the science.

I felt relaxed again, but had barely picked up my pen when there was a call from the Principal's secretary, saying that Mr Jones would like to see me at once.

The Principal sat unsmiling behind a desk cleared of papers, with no bottle or glass on a side shelf. I saw the deputy-principal, a tall, stooping, fifty-cigarettes-a-day man with a face like faded deeds, sitting impassively as a witness. I thought it was something serious if Arthur Reeves was present, as he was usually fully occupied with details of departmental budgets, form filling and all the tasks that the Principal found irksome.

"I haven't heard any alarm bells."

"It's been reported that you behaved in an unseemly manner with a male student in the Weavers, on Saturday. This is an informal meeting, so that I can get an impression of whether the charge has any foundation. If I think it has, I shall have to suspend you and you will have to appear before the Governing Body."

"If you're referring to the pantomime dance, it was just a joke, completely farcical, and to try to turn it into something serious is ridiculous."

"It might be interpreted as improper activity. The problem is what the general public may think of it and what harm that may do to the college. That's my only concern."

I looked at Jones's flickering eyes, knowing that if I weakened, the Principal's gaze would grow confident and malicious. I had behaved foolishly in front of Ugly Bill, who had seized on the chance to make mischief for him, but this was not the time to admit to mistakes. The penalty would be suspension, and the next step resignation from the union post, as the sexual innuendoes spread across the college. I knew I had to fight back, as best I could, as Lumpy or Hairy would have done, not to mention Edward.

"I can't accept any of this. It was an innocent caper, and my problem is that if I persuade the students to give evidence at any proceedings, there will be a risk of a rumour of scandal getting back to Delhi, or wherever. That would finish them over there. They would have no career or prospects of any kind in their own country.

"On the other hand, there would be a tremendous row if the charges were seen as invented so as to get at me for fraternising with Asian students. Any suggestion of racialism could really harm the college, not to mention your career. But there's something else I'd like to talk about - in private, if you don't mind."

"Mr Reeves is deputy-principal and has the right to hear all you say."

"Just as you like, so long as you don't mind what comes out in the wash."

Jones thought for a moment and then nodded to Reeves, who promptly left the room, like the serving man he was.

"Well, Joe? Get on with it."

"It's nothing you aren't aware of. You remember when I had that embarrassing meeting with you in the hotel? If you suspend me, I shall say I suspect you are trying to smear me, to get your own back."

My first thought was that Jones was about to hit me, when he went white and half rose from his chair, until his self-control returned.

"Are you sure, Joe, that you could back up your absurd charge? Does your former
close associate in the Union support you? I don't think so. Who else is there? No –one. The Governors would conclude that you have a very reckless and vindictive side to your nature."

I wondered whether the bright purple of Jones' face indicated bluffing, or an imminent seizure. After a few moments, in which the Principal's colour lost its incandescence, I replied, "If you want to find out who is believable, you'll have to put it to the test."

"All right. There is one more thing. I have also had a report of your escapade in a London pub. Frankly, when I first heard of it, I thought it was just a tipsy public row. I have now been told that you fought with some members of the reserves forces, who had been talking to you about Suez. I know it's a subject on which you have notoriously unpatriotic opinions. I gather that the police have not made a final decision on whether to press charges, but they thought I should know about the fracas, and I shall, of course, take it into account, if I put your case before the Governors."

"The report was all lies. Am I free to go?"

"Yes. You'll be hearing from me."

I sprawled on the settee and asked my painted ladies, "Do you think Special Branch could have advised Jones to tarnish my name, or even sack me? What do you think of my chances? Am I flattened, and out for the count? Would you think it possible

132

it 'slinked to my earlier misfortunes with the car?"

The lady in blue seemed to put down her mandolin, frown at me and say, "Joe, don't let them get you down."

"Thanks for your encouragement, girl on the wall. You'd better go on playing your music. Otherwise you'll break your friend's rapture, and then we won't be a happy household. I've got no time to lose. I'd better start by giving Trevor a ring."

My old friend's response was much as I had feared. "I can see you're in a tricky situation, Joe, but you told me nothing about catching Mr Jones in a compromising situation. I'm not saying it didn't happen, but how could I be a witness for you, when I wasn't there?"

"Well, Jones dropped the plan for a Department of Communication Studies. How do you think that came about? I know you didn't see them in their underwear but that isn't crucial. You could tell the Governors the news I gave you at the hotel. Everyone who knows Jones will understand there must have been something more persuasive than my arguments to get him to change his mind."

"Joe, I can't say anything that implies any connection between what you said about the department and what you're saying now about Mr Jones and Kathleen."

When I heard the sound of Margaret calling out in the background, I guessed it +would be Trevor's cue to ring off, and I was right. I thought of our arid exchange, and the absence of sympathy from Trevor. Jones was sure of him – they'd probably put their heads together, before he was interviewed.

The next morning in the refectory, I was carrying my bacon sandwich to a table, when Teja approached me, his unshaven face looking agitated, and his shiny black hair awry, as he said, "What the hell's going on, sir? That despicable man in the pub is spreading a rumour that you have been carpeted by the Principal on account of my silly game on Saturday. Is it true?"

"Thank you very much for your concern."

Careful not to seem to be trying to influence him, I said in a matter-of-fact manner, "I didn't act very wisely. Little things can seem big things to people who want to create trouble – I'm talking about the pub landlord."

"Yes, sir, but what happens now? Does nonsense affect your career? We will protest to Jones if you get into trouble. We will get support from other overseas students. You are the most helpful lecturer on our course. It is a matter of honour for us to tell him the truth and help you to remove yourself from the hook."

I laughed at the expression and said, "I'm not hooked, not yet, in these murky waters. But thank you very much, I shall have to see if I am hauled into the net."

I shook hands with Teja and Joginder, who had joined us, and my spirits rose, as I jumped three stairs at a time up to the first-floor staff room, where I paused outside the door, saying to myself with mock solemnity, "M'Lord, the Crown is accusing this man of an incestuous relationship, a public homosexual display, an affray in a London pub, opposition to Her Majesty's foreign policy – and a catalogue of other offences that will be disclosed later."

Five minutes later, feeling that my colleagues were perhaps looking at me, I began to keep half an eye open to check if they were making surreptitious glances, but I didn't see any and warned myself against becoming paranoid.

It was soon time for the lunch-time union meeting in the College lecture theatre, where I pulled up a chair behind the table on the stage, beside Tony and Polly. As a Trotskyite socialist, she gave as good as got in good-humoured political banter with me.

"Joe, you're looking good. Anybody would think you'd won the pools. If so, why not buy the college and establish your workers' collective?

"I'll check my coupon with extra care on Saturday night, and if it's a winner, you're on. The new college must have an inscription on the frontage – Socialism In Our Time. The only thing is whether we'll have any students."

"I certainly will – I'm not sure about you."

I grinned and turned to Tony: "She's going to put a motion up for debate: 'That this branch affiliates to the Fourth International'."

"What's that?" said Tony. "England versus Spain, at Wembley?"

"Yes, I'll get you a ticket."

I was getting to know Tony better, since he agreed to take on Trevor's job. He had said then, "The Principal would be able to anything he liked, if we weren't organised. He can still do seventy-five per cent of what he wants, but he has to take us into account after that."

I got through the business fairly quickly. The equal pay policies had been applied to the salary scales, but there was a feeling that it had become harder for women to achieve promotion. Polly spoke fluently. "There's still discrimination. They think they can get away with it, now that women have had a rise. But if women are stuck on the basic scale, while men get promoted because they're men, it's still wrong."

"Not all men are men," someone at the back said softly but audibly. There was another murmur of "Poofters!" from the same quarter.

I stood up, feeling enraged. "That's disgusting talk. A trade union can't tolerate abusive expressions like that, stirring up ridicule and hatred of individuals, just because their private behaviour is different from that of most people. It's out of order, and I won't allow it. If anyone thinks I've got it wrong, I'm sure the union nationally will support my ruling."

I let my voice rise to a bellow, as my conviction grew that I was the target of an attack. "If the cowardly so and so sheltering in the body of the hall would care to show himself, we can have this argument man to man. Otherwise I suggest he shut his mouth and we'll get on with our business."

I waited for the reaction of the meeting, and felt relieved when the clapping was fairly loud. The rest of the agenda was humdrum, focussing on contracts and overtime payments, and when it was over, Polly came up to me and took my arm. She said, "I can imagine what you are going through, Joe. I've heard a rumour, which of course I don't believe, after our private talks in the Cotswolds, but if it had been true it would have been your business and nobody else's."

I allowed her to lead me out of the hall and down to the College lake, where a cacophony arose from the ducks that had swum to the side as we approached. I told her how the story had arisen, and how he was afraid that some of it might stick. He watched her features become scarlet with indignation.

"So it's that swine in the pub who started it. It's his fascist instinct to scapegoat minorities. He needs a good thrashing."

"That wouldn't help. It would only make the rumours seem true."

"Well, there's away in which you can contradict them."

"What's that?

"We can shelve for the time being our differences over whether Russia is state-capitalist and concentrate on salvaging your heterosexual reputation."

She turned her face up to mine and gave me a gentle, moist kiss on the lips. Her pale cheeks, beneath large, dark eyes, turned slightly pink.

"Let's go to the Scala to-night," Joey boy. The film on is right for the occasion. It's *The Witches of Salem.* It'll cheer you up."

We met at the cinema she put my hand on mine when we were in our seats, saying
"You know, Joe, you're being witch-hunted by mistake or more likely by deliberate intent. If they

were to go after me, they'd be right about my sexuality but just as
intolerant and dirty-minded as they are about you."

"O.K. We are doing each other a good turn. By the way, do you think it's any better in Russia?"

"Not a hope. Your workers' state won't accept that we are as we are. We can't be different. They'd send me on a re-education programme, if not to prison."

"I'm sorry they're so backward. It's wrong, whether it's over there or over here."

I insisted on giving her a lift back to her home deep in the suburbs, and we parted with a good handshake. I liked her company and felt in tune with her relaxed temperament and her general political principles. It was a pity from my point of view that she was a lesbian but I kept my disappointment to myself. I drove home, feeling grateful to her for her support, and wondering what my Matisse ladies got up to when I was away.

CHAPTER 12

Saturday morning was running away again, and I felt dissatisfied after spending hours on the newspapers, without coming across anything really worth the time All it took was one really imaginative, original essay or piece of reportage that stayed in the mind. Eisenhower's speech said the obvious - the British Empire was finished, it was the turn of the Americans. But they were going to sell Britain Honest John missiles – what a revolting name!

However, I saw a heading – *Catalogue of Mistakes* - in a middle-opinion paper that had been on the side of Anthony Nutting and Edward Boyle, when they had resigned from Eden's government after the military action. There was a column in the paper listing the main events in the Suez crisis:

July 26, Egypt nationalised the Suez Canal. The British Government, which managed the Canal and had a stake in its ownership, said it was a vital international resource that could be ruined by incompetent Egyptian control. The armed forces were mobilised. Eden saw General Nasser as a Mussolini figure in league with Russia, aiming to eject the West from the Middle East. Gaitskell compared Nasser with Hitler.

August: Collaboration with France underway. The Cabinet was divided and support from the Labour Party ebbed away in favour of diplomatic action through the United Nations.

October 14: the idea of Israel as a secret ally agreed at a meeting at Chequers. Undercover meetings in Paris.

October 22-3: secret meetings at Sevres with the Israeli Premier Ben Gurion. Plans drawn up for Israel to attack Egypt. Britain and France would then tell both sides to stop hostilities and withdraw from the Canal. If Egypt did not comply, as it was certain not to, Britain and France would occupy the Canal Zone (Part of the bargain, according to French reports, was French supply of materials for Israeli nuclear research). Cairo and Port Said bombed when the Anglo-French ultimatum expired.

October 30: Israel launched its attack.

November 5: British forces landed, occupied part of the Canal Zone, and bombed Cairo.

A great outcry throughout the world in the next few days. At the United Nations Britain, denounced as an aggressor, lost the vote by 64 to 5. The Americans inspired a run on the pound that could have produced a sterling crisis worse than the one in 1947.

November 8: the British Government declared a ceasefire.

December 22: the last British troops left the Canal Zone.

It was a fair summary of events. However, the Principal's list of charges against me was of more immediate concern. I rang the union regional organiser, a man I rated as the essence of cool calculation in negotiations with any management.
I put it to him that it seemed a question of
 victimisation of a Union officer.

"That could be - and I personally would tend to go along with that reading. But before we pull all the stops out, we must think hard about the best way to go. I need to see Jones and weigh up the case he makes."

"All right. Do what you can. I had little faith in it, but couldn't object at this stage to the cautious approach, despite Jones's ability to gain strength from the conciliatory tone of an opponent. It would be possible for me to ask Jenny to be a witness to my liking for women, but the publicity would be unfair. Anyhow, that wasn't the real issue. The aim of my enemies was just to throw mud.

I spent the afternoon with Tony and a few other people, watching the College football team and a Cadbury's side slithering in the mud and shooting wildly at goal. As our attention wandered, I asked him what he thought about the tone of the branch meeting. Tony was more forthright than I had expected. "Homophobia spreads like a contagious disease."

"Sounds like the plague that turned up Derbyshire, three hundred years ago."

"So-called queer bashing - it's more widespread and means people live in fear of revealing their nature."

I looked at him with interest. Doctor's son, member of a church choir, Tony didn't have plums in his mouth, but his pronunciation was immaculate BBC. "How did you reach those unconventional conclusions?"

"I went to a minor public school in where open deviations from the norm were not too uncommon. There was a fairly tolerant atmosphere, until a parent who was a vicar spotted a teacher with his arm round another man in a restaurant and raised such a fuss, the teacher had to resign. It seemed wrong to me then, as it does now. If you are under fire, Joe, you'll have my support."

"Thanks, Tony. Did you ever see the film, *Gentleman's Agreement*, in which a gentile pretends to be a Jew, to flush out the anti-Semitism of his friends? Suppose I agreed with the witch-hunters that I am a homosexual. In fact I am not. But why shouldn't I be, if I'd happened to be born with it in my genes?"

"You'd be asking for big trouble, Joe, as you well know. It won't be safe for anyone to do that for ages, perhaps till sometime in the next century, even though there's talk about changes in the law in a few years' time."

"Well, I could challenge the prejudice outright, in the course of my defence".

"Which would be that you weren't afraid of larking around with the student, because you know you're heterosexual."

"That's true. That's not in doubt."

"There shouldn't be any problem. You've always been well liked in the union. You've got some way-out political principles, but so what? Though I would have thought that when Khrushchev revealed the truth about Stalin, it would have put you off the Soviet Union."

I smiled at the turn in the conversation. "Thanks, again, Tony. As far as the Russians are concerned, I certainly admire many things about them, but I support what's right for this country. "

"Does that mean that only Party candidates stand in general elections?

"Perish the thought! I want to see both socialism and democracy. Don't forget, it took centuries for democracy as we know it to evolve. I hope Khrushchev's speech was the start of a loosening up process in the Soviet Union."

"Tell me - would you like to live in Russia?"

"No. I want a more equal society, but my roots are over here."

"Glad to hear that. We can't afford to lose you, Joe."

"Thanks, Tony. See you next week."

I rose early the following morning and listened to a snatch of the Eroica Symphony as I put on my best sports jacket and flannels, a cream shirt and brown-patterned tie. I was going to drive to London, as the Sunday trains were few and unreliable, owing to maintenance work on the line. I had some spare petrol coupons in my wallet, as well as a packet of Durex, although I was ninety-nine per cent sure that it wouldn't be needed and that I was harbouring a crazy fantasy.

I shivered in the cold air and hoped the car would

spring to life without tedious coaxing. I pulled out the choke and turned the key, until the smell of petrol was intense, but after many more bursts of the whirring motor there was still no ignition, and the battery was growing weary. Half an hour later, cursing the grease on my sleeve,
I was seized by panic. I was too late for the 2.30 train to Paddington, though I would have missed the end of the women's march, even if I had caught it.

A sense of frustration overwhelmed me. What could I tell her? Why didn't I have the car serviced? Starting had been touch and go for weeks. I suppose I was thinking I'd soon be getting rid of it, when I traded it in for the Standard.

When I finally overcame my reluctance to ring her, there was no reply, and I visualised her on a train to London. I switched on the record player and put on *Igor's Lament*, which seemed a parody of my own sorrow, so that I relaxed and even grinned at my predicament. If it's all over, I told myself, you've asked for it. You'll have to move on. Only don't blame the hyenas.

After another vain call that evening, I went on impulse to see Rock Around the Clock, which cheered me up. It was mindless but high-spirited, and it's what I felt needed just then.

On the way out I met Trevor with Margaret, who didn't seem to know that relations between Trevor and me had altered.

"Where have you been?" she said severely. "We haven't seen you since Christmas, which was hilarious, looking back at it, though a bit difficult at times."

144

"Jacky and I are no longer an item." I smiled back at her, and added as I glanced at her figure, "When is the baby due?"

"Hasn't he kept you posted?" She looked reproachfully at her husband. "It's in three weeks' time. I wondered actually if the rock 'n roll was going to shock me into an early delivery."

Trevor caught hold of my hand and dragged him into a jive routine on the pavement, and further played up to her impression of normality in his reply: "I mention dates, but he's got such a one-track mind, he thinks I'm referring to Union meetings."

"Make sure you don't miss the christening," Margaret added. "Bring your new girl along - you're bound to have one."

"I thought I had, but it was all a big mistake."

"Two or three will soon be along – like the buses. Come on Trev, let's get our number eight. We don't want to walk home."

She blew me a kiss as they strolled off. Trevor said, "Thanks Joe. See you."

"See you, Trev."

I was glad we were on good terms, but guessed that Trevor hadn't told Margaret about the cooling of the friendship, perhaps to stop her unravelling the truth about Kathleen and Jones. It might be unpalatable to someone with her chapel upbringing and it could make things difficult when she and Trevor met the Principal socially. But I saw I was perhaps too cynical. Trev might want to salvage our friendship. I hoped we could patch things up.

I reckoned it had been one of the least profitable days I could remember - even including Sundays as a teenager, when after finishing off an essay I used to wander round the town, window-shopping or peering at girls seated at stools in milk bars, with their skirts pulled tight over swelling thighs.

Feeling a need to meet some more people, and perhaps get drunk, I called in to the Student Union bar, which was sometimes visited by the younger lecturers, perhaps men seeking a non-academic relationship with women students, though if they were successful it would be pursued elsewhere.

I saw Polly and Tony gyrating out of time to a Bill Haley number blasted through a distorted loudspeaker. They paused when they saw me, more from embarrassment than exertion, and the three of us sat down for a drink.

"I like to keep up some social contact with the students," Polly said.

"Me too," Tony added quickly. "We are friends, and I think you know why that is the right word."

"Sounds good to me," I said, as I quickly downed a pint and stood up to go for a replacement. Seeing the student Li waving to me from the other side of the hall, I excused myself from the table and went to have a word with her. She was with two girls from Malaysia, and the three of them invited me to dance with them. I did little except push forward one arm and shoulder after the other, in time to the beat rhythm, with Li smiling at me most of the time.

The students sitting by the bar clapped me, the men with their slacks pulled up to show off their fluorescent socks.

"Cool for Cats!" I shouted at them, prompting Polly to say when he went back to the table for his drink, "You'll soon recover your heterosexual status, at this rate."

"I don't know that I intend to. Tony will tell you about our talk, yesterday."

"Very well, I shan't ask you to dance. Come on, Tony, let's make a poor attempt to do the *Twist.*"

I smiled back, hoping she sounded a little piqued by my lack of attention to her. Then I bought a round of bottled beers and one double whisky, which I drank quickly. Five minutes later, with a new absence of restraint, I asked Polly for a dance and more or less stayed in time, as a record blared the stomping music of a skiffle band. I raucously sang along to it, but when the music stopped felt I was on the edge of making a fool of myself and walked carefully back to the table, where I sat down feeling I did not belong and missing Jenny and even Jacky. Suddenly, I gave an apologetic shrug of the shoulders, and said, "I'm really starting to feel sorry for myself, so it's bedtime for Joe. Goodnight, campers, see you in the morning."

Waving my half-full bottle, I went outside before finishing the beer with one gulp. Then I hurled the bottle as high into the air as I could. It crashed onto the pavement but I couldn't see the fragments. Someone stepped from the shadows and said with a Belfast accent, "If an Irishman had done that, there'd have been a policeman on hand to take him in."

"You're right," I said morosely. "Maybe I want to be taken in. I feel I'm a low achiever and need shock treatment to liven up my ideas. Also, I'm a little drunk."

147

"Stupid bastard! Take yourself off to bed."

"You're right," I mumbled. Much later, I fumbled with the key in the lock of my front door and fell asleep on the settee, waking in the grey, early light with a hangover, but with time for another hour's sleep in bed. I heard the post arrive, but lay still for a while, feeling thankful that Polly and Tony had not been witness when I had made a late-night exhibition of myself.

At last I collected my only letter and saw Jenny's round hand, as well as the London postmark. She must have posted it at the central sorting office. I carried it round my flat for as long as my patience could stretch, but when it finally broke, I tore open the envelope. It was just as I had feared:

Dear Joe,

        We have just had a good march, followed by a meeting. I am now having some tea in the cafe I referred to. In a way, I am relieved that you did not turn up. As you know, we have no future as a couple, and any anticipated pleasure of your brotherly company was probably a dangerous emotion which might have led us backward into the kind of relationship that had to be avoided.

I am sure you have a good excuse prepared for missing the march. I shall not be making any further arrangement with you. My friend Robert invited me some time ago to go with him on holiday to Russia, and I have decided to accept. I very much look forward to seeing it for myself, instead of through the eyes of others.

My friend is strongly opposed to the system, and it will be interesting to see if either of us is converted to the other's point of view.

I hope you have success in all your endeavours, and get the better of the hyenas. I wish you well.

Jenny

The disappointment numbed me, and the feeling stayed throughout the morning, during which I was aware that my teaching was uninspired and failed to inspire responses from the students. Then I went for a fast walk along the river bank and as I shed tears, the wind blew them away, but they were followed by others. She would probably marry her new man, and I would be shut out of her life for ever. The thought was unbearable.

A day or two later I replied to her letter:

If I had trained as a mechanic or just bothered to learn a few things about cars, I would have made it to London. It will be exciting to see a country where Clause IV of the Labour Party's constitution has been put into practice, even though it isn't paradise, and I'm not sure that ageing ladies should be sweeping the streets, irrespective of the general theory of the equality of the sexes.

Before we met again last autumn, I used to speculate that you were by that time a mother, taking your children on the school run, planning the annual holiday on the beach, talking over with your husband about family arrangements at Christmas, and wondering whether and when you should go back to nursing. All the ordinary things we might have done together. I hope they come true for you.

I am keeping in touch with current politics. I am making a trip soon, for the second time, with college friends and hopefully members of a women's group to look for an underground base where VIPs will take shelter, in the event of a nuclear war. It could make the headlines.

CHAPTER 13

Faint curls of smoke drifted over the crematorium. Mother was sitting red-eyed in the Morris, when I returned from the red brick chapel.

"Hairy's turn in twenty minutes from now," I said. There's an agenda pinned to the door."

"You make it seem like a meeting." The voice arose faintly from her crumpled figure.

"Well, I said, "in a way, it is - his last."

She was past sixty, looking her age, but still unlined. It made me feel very youthful. She was still working in the office at the local Co-op, where they had taken her on full-time after Edward died.

She made no response to my comments.

"Try not to be sad, mom," I said at last. "It's a natural process. It's the finish for Hairy. All we can do is to praise his life. You always told me there was no pie in the sky."

I was a young child again and the man in the next street drank a bottle of disinfectant and mother was saying they were putting him into an orange box and that was that.

I smiled at her. Should I have brought her to this bleak Victorian burial ground and the crematorium? Generations of industrial workers lay here, as they once stood side by side at their machines in the factories. Or as they used to sit together in the lounges and bars of the big city pubs. Except that there's no closing time, only natural decay. But I can't depress her with these thoughts.

"Perhaps you shouldn't have come to another funeral of the old comrades," I said gently. "I remember bringing you to Lumpy's, two years ago. But I'm glad to come with you to see them off. They made quite an impression on me, as well. I last met Hairy some time ago, when he was clipping tickets on the train bringing me back from London to Birmingham."

I remembered the lean figure, and the mottled, ageing face staring at me. Then the words tumbled out: "Blow me, you must be Joe. How are you? You haven't changed much in your features since I saw you last. It was the beginning of the war, just before the Great Western sent me to Devon. Now I'm thinking about retirement, though it's still a few years away. Where has the time gone? It's thirteen or fourteen years since you lost your father. He was always very principled in his political beliefs. He could have stayed in his reserved occupation and been alive today."

By this time, everyone in the compartment was looking at us and I thought it would be a long session of reminiscences as Hairy continued, "In those days, I used to think Jerusalem was just over the hill, or would be, when the war was over."

I replied, "We're still in the foothills and the hyenas are still out there."

We both laughed, and Hairy said, "We're making some progress, though. Attlee did a good job in some ways. It's a step forward for the railways to be taken over. As for the Soviet Union, they must still be exhausted after their fantastic war effort."

Then he smiled at the other passengers and wished me the best of luck, before moving on to clip some more tickets.

I came back to the present when Dorothy began to talk about the meetings that took place in her living room throughout my childhood. She ended rhetorically, "Where would we have been without the Soviet Union in the war?"

I nodded. I was sure she was thinking of the newsreel shot of the Russian soldiers unfurling the red flag over what remained of the Reichstag. No doubt it was printed on the memories of this straggly group of elderly mourners gathered here in their shabby overcoats. Coming to funerals must seem to them like a series of rehearsals for the final shows in which each one in turn will have the main part.

Scanning the wasted faces, I thought I could recall one or two from my early years, though they all must have known Hairy as a political activist, or perhaps worked with him on the railways.

We entered the chapel, to a muffled sound of the Eroica, played on a crackly record behind the scenes. The Humanist speaker, a gaunt man, summarised Hairy's trade union and political career, making a short reference to the International Brigade, and said that he was a leaf fallen from the tree of life. I could have told him that Hairy was well over forty when he went to Spain, but came home sporting a Basque beret with boyish enthusiasm, confessing how surprised he was when he discovered that a tree did not stop a bullet. I said I would never forget that useful information. Mother had never known that Hairy had admired the achievements of the Labour Government after the war. She wouldn't have agreed with the praise, any more than she was impressed by Khrushchev, who had just lifted the covers off Stalin.

Finally, the gaunt man pulled a lever and Hairy slid along the lines for the last time. We left to a burst of The Red Flag, and I saw many pairs of red, moist eyes amongst the mourners, as the undertakers shepherded them out briskly, so as to make way for the next item on the agenda. They were sad but also perhaps thankful that so much of the experience of the past that they were remembering was no longer being inflicted on their children.

I drove mother back to the council estate on the edge of Birmingham. The living room had the radiogram that she had saved up for after the war, and a new rug covered part of the lino. The draught that I remembered still came from under the door and was partly combated by a silk stocking stuffed with rags, pressed against the gap. The longer I stood on the hearth, the more he conjured up old images. Mother on her knees lighting the screwed up paper, sticks of wood and charred coals. Mother shouting at the big boys who threatened me. Myself aged six, running to tell dad the men in suits were in the Crescent, checking wireless licences, and dad coolly telling the men that they could not come in without a warrant. Then there was the bent figure of Old Arthur from next door, who could fix copper wire so as to by-pass his electric meter .

Then it was wartime, and I was in grammar school clothes, growing away from the boys of the Crescent, and the family had for the first time both a steady wage and a week at the seaside. My lifelong impressions of the holiday were a blinding sandstorm, their landlady creating a suspicion that she was running us down when she spoke in Welsh to her friends, and the talk about Edward's desire to join the army. He had tried before, and I remembered Dorothy's anxiety, as well as her admiration of his courage.

Mother called me inside, and we had tinned salmon, mashed potatoes and peas, a traditional quick meal. Then I went home, where the sun touched the *Magic* picture and made it blaze against the white wall. I waved at the large, girls in the painting, with the two circles on each chest and wished they would step onto his carpet and say, "Hallo, Joe," like the sisters I never had. I had often felt envy of my father for having grown up in a large family.

The family was now scattered, the most distant being Mary and her husband, who emigrated to Australia after the war. At ninety, Grandma lived alone, in a cluttered bed-sitting room on the ground floor of the old house, though a nurse visited her and a carer did her shopping and paid her bills.

The last time I had visited her, she said, "Your Dad and Granddad kept their lips sealed about many things, but they didn't give up when they put their mind to something. You're like them. Look at the way you come round to see me. I see you more than I see your mother."

I could see her steadying herself on her metal stick and picking her way forward to the door, as though stepping from one stone to another across a stream. Two years earlier she had smashed her ankle, when the large dog she then kept had pulled her over in the park. After a few days in hospital she was taken to a nursing home, where the matron made her empty her handbag.

It was one of Grandma's favourite stories. "She took away my lighter, as though I was a child. That was enough. I wouldn't have a cup of tea, so they couldn't tranquillise me. I would have been gaga in no time, like the others. I insisted in coming home. You came with Dorothy and helped me to get out."

I was always fascinated by the thin bone of her wrists and the mottled red and purple of her foot, where the bones were stuck together again. Her face was bloated, with a shapeless nose and a light covering of straggly hair, like seedlings. I hardly dare look at the handsome features of the portrait standing on the bookcase next to the commode. Her stucco had crumbled in the sixty-odd years since the sepia was taken. I wondered how long it would be before her clearance order arrived.

When I last saw her, she had turned luminous eyes on me and said, "Joe, the nurse who washes me told the doctor about the lump on my back. He has advised me to have it looked at in the hospital. It could be malignant."

I had been indignant. "Why are you at home? Why didn't you let us know? I'll ring the surgery myself now."

She had looked at me fondly, then adding casually, "I told him I wouldn't think of it. I've lived with this lump for years. If there is malignancy, then at least it's lying low. Once they use the knife, anything could happen. The cancer could race round my body, and then where would I be?"

She had paused for me to give silent assent to her logic, before continuing, "The woman next door said my sherry is cheaper in the Co-op this week. Dr Mellows says it's much better than sleeping pills."

I had pushed her in her wheelchair to the Co-op, where she had insisted on hobbling into the shop, so that she could chat to as many people as possible, carefully mentioning that she was ninety. She watched every reaction in their faces and increased the intensity of her speech if there was any sign of restlessness. They all stayed rooted to the shop floor. There was rarely a mutiny against the tyranny of the weak. Companionship was a drink, which she took in great draughts to last for the days when she saw no one. I sometimes found her hunched in her chair, with vacant gaze, lower lip drooping and a feeble, high-pitched voice saying, "What's the point of going on like this? I'm ready to go at any time. I've no fear of dying." Half an hour later, she would make me a cup of tea, and her voice would be firm, her face animated and pink. She would recite all the old litanies of stories of childhood, her career raising six children, and Granddad's desertion just after his fiftieth birthday. Old age had crept up on her like twilight slowly dimming the afternoon.

Later on I went down to the Weavers, to meet Trevor. We both needed the companionship, but were more circumspect in our conversation than we used to be, before his promotion. I mentioned I had been with my mother to the funeral of an old family friend.

"Sorry to hear it. I try to avoid those melancholy occasions."

"The man who was cremated was one of several friends of the family who had a big effect on me when I was a child. Childhood experiences don't fade easily, but the world changes. I went for a walk on the new council estate and saw all those bright houses and wide roads. There were lots of young people about, in new suits and nice dresses. It seemed as though the revolution had happened, and I hadn't noticed it."

"Ah, this is the chance I've been waiting for. Perhaps you should join me in the Labour Party.

"Perhaps I should think about it. At least, after some hesitation, they were against military action over Suez. But there's still something holding me back. Anything that makes life better for ordinary people must be a good thing. Sooner or later though, living within the system won't be enough. It will have to go, but don't ask me when or how."

"Well, you've got your dreams, but not political power. In the meantime, the Labour Party has a good chance of getting hold of that at the next election."

"Not realty. It has never challenged real power - the power of capital. But I agree, Labour in Downing St would be a step forward. The danger is we turn our back on the politics of the left. You know - socialists buy houses, spend their time decorating and gardening, and end up voting Tory."

"No chance. Labour will be back at the next election. At least, there'll never be political apathy in our house, since my wife is a spirited Welshwoman, though unfortunately she's not a socialist."

I went to the bar to refill our glasses with Ansells bitter. When I sat down again, Trevor changed the subject. "My problems are not political. Margaret persuaded me to take out the two and a half thousand pound mortgage on the new bungalow."

"So?"

"That's a lot of money. My father's house cost less than two hundred, only twenty or so years ago."

"If I'm toying with the idea of getting a new Standard Ten, you can buy a bungalow. There's full employment today. If you lose your job, it isn't too difficult to get another one. We can't forget the past. We just have to say, "Never again.""

Seeing the relaxed look that had spread over Trevor's features, now he had been given the moral support he wanted, I said cheerfully, "Look on the bright side, Trev. You'll be having a baby next, and you'll call him David Lloyd, if it's a boy, since you're married to a Liberal."

"Margaret wants a girl."

"Perhaps she'll at least call her after" - he stopped himself from saying 'Jenny' - but added "'Nye's wife."

"I doubt it, as she's not a Labour woman. She comes from a hill farm in the north of Wales. We don't talk politics much."

"Well, you'll be doing your bit for Britain. I feel very envious. I should like to be buying a house and starting a family. I don't have a problem in finding a girl. It's fine in the short run, but doesn't work out in the long run."

"That sounds like an economist talking. What you need is a passionate affair to cheer you up."

"Maybe. If I let the grass grow under my feet, I won't be a true member of my father's family."

"Well, Hamlet, beware of the ghosts on the college staircase, if not the ramparts, when you're working late. They may come to remonstrate with you for being a bit tardy in love, if not in politics. A good affair will help you to get over Julie."

"Thank you, Horatio. I expect my celibacy is only temporary. If Granddad were still alive, he'd say, "Never mind about Julie, or Kate or Mary. The world is teeming with lovely girls, with breasts like the peaks of Snowdonia."

"Trevor laughed. "I used to think like that," he said. "But I wouldn't say that to Margaret, today. I shouldn't think you believe in it, either."

"No, it's a bit like my Granddad's conceited attitude to women, when he said they were pebbles on the beach just waiting to be picked up by men. He impressed me when I was fifteen. Now I know that finding the right person isn't so easy and that a man is just as likely to be a pebble on the beach, picked up and then thrown away by a woman."

"True. I suggested not long ago that you visit Russia and find a lovely girl. She might even be the soul mate you're really looking for."

I did not reply at once. I couldn't tell Trevor that I have constant desire to meet someone. He's forgotten what it feels like. I suppose I could mention Jenny, but there's not much point in confessing love for a girl I can never live with. I said, "I like the idea. Nadia and I will go walking in the Lenin Hills, overlooking Moscow University. It sounds quite romantic but it's probably an illusion. There's probably more concrete than greenery."

At home, I ate a pork pie and drank a whisky, before falling into bed. I half woke up in the early hours in a panic, tightly wrapped in bedclothes on the floor. I had had a dream, which had not yet faded away. I was on a train chugging into the countryside, with the heat from bodies sticking to me in the crowded compartment, and a strong smell of vegetables and live chickens rising from the baskets on the floor by a knot of peasant women. One of them pulled her blouse down below a brown breast, as I was eyeing her figure, and they all shrieked with laughter.

When the train stopped by a village square, I looked out at yellow-grey walls, with blazing geraniums in front of them and the silver mountain peaks in the distance. Gypsy fiddlers were playing *Hora Staccato,* and girls in ornate costumes were wandering around, rehearsing songs. I climbed down for a drink from a samovar standing on a table, and seeing the voluptuous blonde girl serving him, said, "You remind me of Marilyn."

She replied in English, with a rising intonation, "I sometimes think I should like to be paid a fortune for letting men weave their fantasies around me, but I live in the real world."

The shining eyes were an invitation and the pouted lips a come-on, as she picked up a glass, filled it with red wine and kissed the rim, before handing it to me, saying "This is our best Georgian Sauvignon, just for you."

I stammered my thanks, and an electric charge ran through me when she put her mouth to his ear and whispered, "I am Natasha."

"I am Joe. Can we meet again?"

"Stay in the hotel and wait for me."

A genial, middle-aged man led me to a hotel and beckoned to him to enter, but I decided to saunter through the village, past the huge posters of Lenin and Khrushchev. Then my head was thumping and I felt sick. I was lying on his back, arms tethered above my head. Bars of light were cast on the floor by the sun shining through a high grill in the wall. Bottles of wine lay in racks near me. A door opened and a short man with a black moustache resembling Stalin's came in, accompanied by two young men wearing folk costume.

I was marched up some stairs from the cellar into the hall of the hotel to which he had been shown, and into the square, where the crowd enfolded us. One of the young men waved a bottle of vodka in the air, as though they were on a drinking spree. I knew my captors would say I was drunk if I struggled, and even if I could break their grip, they might hit me on the head with the bottle.

A chance of release came sooner than I expected. A grey van hurtled over the cobbles, with horn blaring. It forced a path through the crowd and stopped two metres away. I was dragged towards it, but as one of the men opened the door his hold weakened. Freeing one arm, I drove my fist into the man's face, and as he reeled, I shook my other arm free and ran into the crowd, forcing myself along a zigzag path, until the stage loomed in front of me and the general noise was drowned by the sound of a large choir singing in hard, clear, passionate, peasant tones.

A shot rang out some distance away. The crowd writhed like a snake, as the part nearest the firing backed away. My hand was seized, and I saw it was Natasha, who pulled me into an alley and a maze of narrow streets, through a side door and into a terraced house. She said, "You are in great danger. The old guard want to capture you and pretend you are a western spy, in order to discredit Mr Khruschev."

My instinctive reply was to touch her lips with mine. She pressed her body to me and I felt inflamed. But she was no longer blonde Natasha, but stocky and auburn-haired Jenny.

There was the noise of voices and a knock on the door. The adrenaline rose in me and I plunged towards the window, wrenched it open and scrambled over the sill into a yard, pulling Jenny after me. The gate was unlocked and we raced panting along an alley towards the clamour of the square, the fast footfall of their pursuers gaining on us. I thrust Jenny into the safety of the crowd, and then I was trying to free myself from my blankets on the floor of my bedroom. After a struggle, I managed to unwind them, and went into the kitchen to make a cup of coffee, wondering why a dream had to be disillusioning.

I wished I could tell Jenny that I had a dream, or a nightmare, recently, in which I was in Georgia – the one in the USSR, not the one that someone sings is 'on his mind.' There was a siren or temptress – what's new?, you will say – with whom I made good progress, but some bad men kidnapped me, and it all went wrong, except at the end, when she turned into you. But then I woke up. I wished I had kept on dreaming of my sister.

CHAPTER 14

A fantasy dream was all well and good, but the real world of the Government's bolthole in the event of atomic war was preying on my mind. It was the second week in January. Polly was also keyed up with curiosity about what we might discover deep in the Cotswolds. Tony said he would stay away but be ready to brief for the defence in the magistrates' court or publicise our expedition if we did not return.

I had assumed that the Black Sash brigade would be joining us in force. Polly was again shamefaced when she said that support from the women's network would not be forthcoming until they had discussed it at their next monthly meeting. "They are very London-oriented and rather bureaucratic. Everyone is expected to follow the leaders."

I saw that she had banked on reinforcements, as she had on the previous foray, but that a further tide of criticism from me would achieve nothing. It also occurred to me that there were disadvantages in large numbers of screaming people, who could neither   storm the brown doors nor slip inside undetected.

We agreed to go back to the secret base, as we had agreed we would. It was good to have her company but each of us was wrapped in thought and few words were exchanged, until we came to rest in an industrial estate in Bourton. I might have driven to a parking spot much closer to our destination but thought the car would be too conspicuous on a country road if there was trouble and we had to make a run for it.

It was a crisp January morning, seasonally cool, with a delicate lace of frost in the fields when we set out at nine in the morning. But there was no biting wind. Silently we followed the route as before across the damp turf, through gaps in hedges, over gates and down slopes until Naunton was again visible through the trees. The pub was closed but Polly had brought a thermos flask of tea. We set about the second stage of the walk and came to the notice forbidding further access to the quarry. We looked expectantly at each other but neither showing signs of hesitation we continued to the quarry edge and along to the same precipitous path that led us down to the bunch of trees at its foot. I gazed down towards the great doors and started with nervous excitement. They were open, and black boxes evidently unloaded from the helicopter nearby were being carried through the doorway. Two men in RAF uniform climbed down from the aircraft and followed the others indoors. Half-rising to my feet, I was about to go closer to listen to what was being said, when Polly whispered, "Hang on, we're probably on Ministry of Defence land, without permission, so watch out."

"It should be all right now. I'll take a peep inside and if it's safe, I'll wave you over. Don't forget, it'll be damn difficult for us to go back in a hurry the way we came in. There could be a passage leading to another outside door in a field or lane."

I sprinted the forty yards to the doors, which seemed as thick as castle walls, and half put my head round the edge of the nearer one. The sight startled me. I saw a great cavern rising up inside the hill, and a long block of flats on the left side, having doors at intervals, and windows with beige curtains. Outside the building there were train lines, with stationary coaches, lit up by bright lamps, while high up small lights glowed behind the windows of some of the flats.

I waved urgently to Polly and grinned at her anxious face when she came up to me. "It's an urban village under the Cotswolds. It must be the ultimate Government hideaway. These doors are two feet thick, and a hundred feet of rock and earth overhead must make it bombproof."

"Perhaps the men are having a tea-break in one of the flats," Polly said with more confidence. "We could make ourselves known and ask how to find the way out."

"And get locked up for trespassing and stumbling on one of the best kept Government secrets? I think that's more likely than soft words and a sketch map showing us to the door. If we stick to the poorly lit side on the right, we should be able to make our way forward to see what's beyond the flats."

She seemed unconvinced by my spurt of optimism but we both knew that action of some sort was necessary, as the airmen could return at any moment. I was glad that she nodded and even more relieved when we skipped into the shadows and started to walk silently along the wall, counting the steel girders which buttressed it at intervals of about ten feet.

Noisy footsteps and loud talking caused me to cower against a dark patch of wall alongside Polly, while trying to listen to what was being said. I heard snatches of talk about "going up west, tonight," and "getting back in time to see the Arsenal game," and also a more interesting comment – "learn your s'il vous plait and oui, oui" – to which the reply was, "They'll all speak English, don't they?"

Then the engine roared and two remaining men closed and locked the doors. I had felt very certain about my actions so far, but a realisation that there was no retreat dampened my spirits, especially when I saw the distress in Polly's features.

I tried to reassure her. "We'll carry on slowly. Don't worry, I've a feeling we'll be all right." I tried to sound sure of myself as we crept further into the cavern, hugging the wall and trying to hide our faces, while staying alert to any sounds or movement by the building.

I kept the lead position and when we had advanced about a hundred feet was the first to see in the far wall the mouth of a tunnel, with railway lines disappearing into it. I judged we were trapped. But I said to Polly, "See, there's another way out."

"What do you advise now then, Joe? Do we wait for a train and buy a ticket or stow away in a goods wagon? Is Will Hay going to appear on the platform? It's a bit like a film set, except that we don't have parts to play. We could be disposed of and no-one outside would ever know what happened to us."

"Well, Tony would raise the alarm."

"What consolation would that be? He didn't see us enter this underworld. The M.O.D. would flatly deny we had trespassed on their property. The story would get round that you'd been in trouble at work and had walked away from it, or even that we had eloped."

"Okay. But let's not be too alarmist. There would plenty of propaganda countering those tales. At the moment we're hikers exploring the Cotswolds. We came upon the quarry by chance, wandered into the cavern and couldn't get out again. Will someone please open the doors, so we can go on our way?"

But my heart was beating with the force of a cannon and I dreaded the prospect of being hauled before a court for trespass on Ministry property, the colourful write up in the newspapers of my association with Polly and my dismissal from the College.

I was ready for her to tear apart my facile excuses for our presence in the cavern, but when I heard footsteps approaching I held up a cautionary hand. Then I saw a middle-aged man in Air Force uniform staring at us. If the outline of the figure and the shape of the almost bald head seemed familiar, the hoarse voice removed all doubt. "Who do we have here?" the man cried out. Wait a minute! Isn't it? It is, by fuck. It's Corporal Butler!"

"Sergeant Brummit!" I said, amazed, horrified and relieved at the same time, as he stepped forward to meet me. "I don't really believe it. This is a long way from Bridgnorth. Do you work here now?"

"Yes, by fuck, if you can call it work. You know

you're in bloody big trouble, if you're caught here?" He glanced towards Polly, who was still cowering against the wall. "What're you two up to? Been rambling and now looking for a place for nooky?"

"Something like that."

"Well then, listen - I shouldn't be saying this. I shall deny it if you ever tell on me. Most of these flats are empty but furnished. Go through that door over there and up the staircase. Go in one of the rooms. When you see the big doors open again, it'll be up to you to sneak out. If the police get their hands on you, by fuck, it's all up. You'll go to jail for trespass, after they've roughed you up."

I smelled the spirits on Brummit's breath but felt only deep gratitude. "Why are you helping us?" I said.

"'Cause I'm getting demobbed on Tuesday, after twenty years' service. And I knew you for a short time, when you were called up. You did well, by fuck, to stand up for what you believed in, even though you were still wet behind the ears – and probably still are. Now, do as I tell you. You're lucky, because there aren't many on duty here, as a rule, but there's a big show on tomorrow and the place will be swarming with officers with lots of rings...."

"But they've only got one arsehole – I remember the words. Thanks a million."

As Brummit walked on, I turned to Polly. "Come on," I said softly, taking her arm, "I think we'd better do as he says. We need some breathing space."

I pulled her across the well-lit space towards the door, and up a staircase to the second floor, where there was a small landing, with facing doors. A door opened into a hallway, leading to a small kitchen and a plainly furnished living room, with a good quality brown carpet, a three-piece leatherette suite, a table with four wooden chairs and a bookcase. A low light from the lamps shone through the window.

"It's a superior prison," Polly said sadly. "How long will our sentence be?"

"Not long. Brummit was right. We'll keep a lookout from behind the curtains and seize our opportunity."

"It was good of him to help us. We were amazingly lucky to meet a friend of yours."

"He's a heavy drinker and should have a happy retirement, if not a long one. Well, I hope he will be able to control his drinking, for I am indebted to him for his real sense of comradeship

"However, if we were VIPs sent here in an emergency, we would need food fairly quickly. There has to be something to eat in the kitchen."

I investigated, while Polly slumped on the settee. I called out my find:

"What would you say we could expect to see? Perhaps a kettle, tea and teapot, tins of spam, cheese biscuits, marmalade, tinned salmon, tins of soup? Chocolate, sweets, dried milk and various other things?"

"Are you kidding?"

"I'm afraid so. There's sweet nothing to eat. Just the Bible and the works of Shakespeare."

"Joe, you're a sadist. I could swallow a tin of dog's meat – if there was a tin opener."

"As a matter of fact there is, as well as knives,

forks and spoons, and crockery."

After cursing our failure a second time to wait for the pub to open at Naunton, I settled down in an armchair with *Hamlet*, which I sampled listlessly, while Polly curled up on the settee. I resolved to read the soliloquies and to peer out of the window after each one, but it seemed a bizarre occupation in the circumstances and soon gave it up. Thinking about the play, I saw my life's dilemma. Hamlet could either go for a comfortable life at peace with the king or keep his pledge to his father's ghost. Very appropriate – Edward was the ghost playing a similar part in my life. I could spend my life kicking against the pricks, or I could settle with them. Which side was I on? Perhaps I should play for time, like Hamlet, by pretending to be mad. Some would say it was no pretence.

I took a look outside at the desolate frontage, while Polly was gently snoring on the settee. Nothing stirred, but hearing an engine noise in the direction of the tunnel, I ran lightly downstairs, taking care not to slam doors, and dashed over to the shadowy wall.

Going slowly back to the place we reached earlier, I saw that an engine had pulled two carriages from the far end of the tunnel, and a group of people including two women were standing beside it, while an officer in blue shook hands with an elderly man and two younger men, all three wearing dark grey overcoats and trilby hats, as though they were businessmen or government officials. The party then moved off towards the end of the long building and disappeared through a doorway.

"They have very lax security precautions," Polly's voice said behind me. "It wasn't very nice to find you were prepared to leave me in the flat, Joe. Fortunately, I was half-awake and came on your heels."

"I'm sorry. I thought the sleep would do you good. I was coming straight back. Now we're both here, we may as well go over to the coaches. If they're going somewhere, we might be able to hide away."

"Stowaways," she said wistfully – that just might get us out of this hole, back into the sunny meadows and hills. I'll be glad to be back in my place, completely alone."

I thought to myself that our camaraderie seemed to be running down, like a car battery, but concluded "Whatever will be, will be." It was a stressful situation. I said out loud, "Let's do it, now – run, Polly!"

I saw it was an engine without steam. "It's a diesel," I said. Two coaches were for passengers, but I saw the third half full of packing cases, where we could hide fairly easily, if we could get in. I turned the handle, the door opened silently and we scurried inside.

"We were quick as rats on the scent of cheese," I whispered to Polly, as we crouched in the corner.

"Joe, if the escapade of Joe and Polly gets embroidered by the press, it will scotch any false rumours about your sexuality – and true ones about mine."

Half an hour later there were sounds of footsteps and conversation, and then the train started to move. There was a flash of daylight but we quickly entered the tunnel, faintly illumined by yellow lights, and a few minutes passed until we emerged into the bright scenery of the Cotswolds. There was the clatter of changing of lines and soon after that we passed through a simple country station, with a sign saying Charlton Abbots.

"Where do you we're going?" Polly sounded resigned as though she might simply have nodded, if he had said Penzance."

"It could be anywhere,"I replied. "It makes sense, having rail as well as air links to the base. Too many helicopter flights would draw attention to its existence."

"We'll have to make a run for it when we stop," she said. "Then we can get a taxi back to Naunton."

"It's a good idea but will it be as straightforward as that? At some time, they're bound to become more security conscious. We've had it too easy so far"

Ten minutes later, we reached the suburbs of a substantial town and then slowly entered Cheltenham station, avoiding the main platforms and coming to a halt in a deserted siding. Back in hiding, after glimpsing two men in boiler suits who had got down from the engine, I heard them stop at the goods carriage.

"Better lock up," one of them said. "We should do everything by the book, this week-end."

"Who else's coming besides the frogs?"

"I don't know. All I know is the army and air force and probably the bloody navy are in on this one."

There was the sound of a key turning on the door of their coach, and the men moved off, leaving a mixture of feelings racing through my veins. I was as apprehensive as Polly about our safety but also intrigued by what might be happening at the underground base that weekend.

"Is it worth trying to break a window?" she said.

"Not a hope. We should need a hammer and we'd only add damage to property to any other charges to which we're already liable."

I gave her a brotherly bear hug, saying "Once again, we'll just have to wait on events."

We had not waited very long when I heard the sound of a motor and, as I looked out between two packing cases, saw two Jaguars draw up outside. A bevy of army officers assembled by the second car to receive the man who stepped out from it.

I was aghast. "Oh hell! Do you know who that is? I think - though I'm not sure. He's got the flowing white hair."

"Yes, I think I recognise him. I'm Jewish enough to know someone who looks every inch an Israeli leader. My mother talks a lot about him. She worships them all and thinks Israel can do no wrong. It could be Ben-Gurion. We're into something very secret and dangerous. For the first time, I've got real doubts about whether we shall get away."

"Let's not get too despondent. It's only half-past two. If we're taken back in the train to the base, we shall just have to try to get out of this cage – perhaps try hard to break a window as you suggested – and walk along the rail lines out into the fields. I don't know why we didn't think of that before – when we first hid in here."

"We didn't know how far the line went underground. It might have gone on for miles."

As the voices got louder, I said, "Look out, they're probably going to put things in here Get low down."

I heard the lock being opened and cases being piled on the floor of the goods carriage. After that, the lock was turned again and we set off on return journey, which seemed interminable. We sat swaying on cases, until the train entered darkness and came to a . halt in the cavern. I heard the footfalls of people alighting and boxes being moved out, a few feet away from where Polly and I were crouching. I had an extravagant feeling of relief when the door was slammed but not locked again, and Polly said, "We've got to make a run for it. I don't think there'll be another chance."

"Okay, so long as the coast is clear."

I stood up and bent double crept to the door, which I opened slightly and then closed. "There are soldiers with rifles about forty yards away, posted at the entrance to the tunnel. We're still trapped, for the time being."

"I can't stand this any longer, Joe. Besides, I've got toilet needs and can't hold on any longer. I'm sorry, I'm going out. I'll make sure they won't know I was on the train."

"Well, it won't take them long to find me."

"Don't do that, Polly! You'll ruin everything and you'll be at their mercy. They aren't looking this way. Drop off the train and go between the carriages. Show something of the spirit your parents had in Warsaw."

"That's very unfair, Joe. This situation isn't a

176

matter of life or death. Arguably, the base will be better publicised if I'm put on trial for trespass than it will be if we manage to escape. Anyway, they won't know you're here. I'll say I was hiking with a girlfriend, who refused to follow me through the gates this morning. That will give you a chance to hide and look for a way out, later."

I could say no more to influence her. As she carefully opened the carriage door I suddenly thought I would be safer lying under the train, before deciding on another hiding place. The soldiers were looking towards the tunnel, as each of us made a long, silent step down to the road. Polly slipped off silently and after following her I lay down on the ground and crawled under the carriage. There was just enough space, with my head pressed into the soil and gravel, and I hoped I would lie motionless in the unlikely event of the engine moving off. I could hear but not see what was going on. The sound of Polly's footsteps was loud enough, as she approached the sentries, with no more attempt at concealment.

A voice yelled, "Stand still, or I fire! Where the 'ell have you come from?"

"I was out walking and came down into the quarry but found it hard to get out, as I'd hurt my leg. I've been over against the wall since I came in, when the doors were open."

"Bert, sound the alarm. As for you, come with me, you silly bitch. Put your hands behind your back. Right, now you're 'cuffed, you can come and tell your story to the lieutenant."

I heard Polly shout, "Take your hands off me! I've

177

done nothing to justify this arrest!" as she was forced to go with the soldier. I saw my dilemma: reveal myself to the guards, to keep an eye on how she was being treated, and help as best I could, or keep quiet to try to find out what an important person from Israel was doing in Gloucestershire. I did not know what to do for the best. I didn't have a more dependable friend. If she was in physical danger, nothing would hold me back. Would she want me to jump out of hiding to argue with the lieutenant? Would it do any good or even make things worse by showing a second person involved? I decided to stay a bit longer, before going down the train lines and raising some sort of alarm outside the cavern, if Polly was still being held.

I was glad I had got out of the coach, as there were more footsteps and the door-locking sound again. Then it was quiet, and looking out I couldn't see anyone. I reasoned that the two sentries were summoning reinforcements for a search of the cavern, and that it was now or never for my move. Pressing my hands into the earth, I pushed my body forward until I was in between two coaches, lying there eyeing the flats. The nearest flat, at the end of the block, only thirty feet or so from the train, was in darkness, and if its door was not locked would probably offer more shelter of the kind we had found earlier in the day. The soldiers must have taken Polly to one of the other buildings round the corner from the line of flats.

I dashed forward, tried the door handle and felt a surge of joy when it let me inside, at about the same time as a siren went off and a searchlight was turned on the train and the track. The soldiers did not believe that Polly had been on her own. As a dull light fell on the building and came through the windows, I ran up to the top floor and entered one of the apartments. It was a shock to see clothes spread out on the sofa, a three-part empty bottle of red wine on the table and suitcases on the floor. There was no sound of anyone, and after a survey on tiptoe I was sure I was alone.

I went into the kitchen to grab some food – anything edible, but there was nothing. The other flats on the staircase might also have occupants. I could go outside again, but would probably find my way into the tunnel blocked by now. Or I could try to hide again, inside the flat. I looked at the trap door on the small landing and knew what I had to do. With one foot on the handrail and another on the knob of the bedroom door handle, I could shift the cover. I stood irresolute for a minute before taking my weight on my forearms and hoisting myself free of the supports and starting a desperate struggle to haul myself into the loft before my strength ran out. One and then both upper arms were over the edge of the opening and after more flaying of my legs and furious panting, I pulled himself up and lay across the joists for some time, before carefully replacing the cover of the trap door.

I felt a sense of triumph, until I heard footsteps coming up the stairs, all the way to the top. I lay almost without breathing, but then became alert, as I realised I could hear every word of the conversation between a man and a woman who had come into my flat.

CHAPTER 15

With stale air in my nostrils but resisting the urge to sneeze, I steadied myself on the hard joists, for fear of crashing through the ceiling of the room below and falling at the feet of the two people who had just come in. As I had left the cover over the entrance very slightly out of place, I could clearly hear a man and a woman, talking languidly, with an exaggerated drawl from the woman, as though she were auditioning for a part in a West-End comedy.

"Dar-ling, that was an easy time we had in there. I thought we should be at it hammer and tongs, till you perspired and I glowed."

"Yes, pet, the Jews didn't want to show their cards too soon. They're waiting for our top men to meet them this evening."

"Why couldn't they have met them in Whitehall? We could have got away to the club by midnight. What's the point of coming to this ghastly cave?"

"Absolute top security. If we breathe a word about this, even to Nigel and Michael or Angela, off we go to prison. It'd be even worse than Roedean."

"It isn't even as if we're in the bloody countryside. It's more like being in a Pharaoh's tomb. What's the point, dar-ling? Does anyone think the Russians are going to atom-bomb us this week-end?"

"Elizabeth, they just don't want a word to get out about a hush-hush meeting with the Jews.

Anywhere in London or a country house would be leaked out or spotted by some nosey reporter."

"I guess you're right. Let's unpack the food. How about coffee, ham and eggs?"

I felt faint when I heard their clatter in the kitchen and smelled the fried food. I tried to think what I could do, perhaps staying indefinitely, climbing down to the kitchen and bathroom when they were out, and then retreating to my hideout.

Eventually, they left the apartment and I heard them go downstairs. I considered my choices: explore or escape. I landed heavily on the floor and then stood on a chair to replace the cover of the trapdoor. I found some bread and ate like a wolf, before looking through the briefcases of the two people, whom I took to be typists or technical workers of some description. There was a passport in the name of James Norton, but I hardly saw my own features in the portrait. Norton was thin-faced and dark, while I was full-cheeked and fair. But some Ministry of Defence papers with Norton's name and address, and work location as an interpreter might be useful.

I was attracted to the wardrobe, in which there was a grey suit and several shirts and ties, all presumably belonging to Norton. Impetuously, I changed into these clothes, which fitted reasonably well, even if the shirt collar was too tight. The trousers were about the right length, though very tight round the waist and the jacket was all right, if I kept it unbuttoned.

I picked up a few sheets of foolscap paper from the table and rolled them up to look like a document

I was delivering somewhere. Then I walked to the end of the block, trying to look unselfconscious and professional, and nodded to a sentry, before turning the corner and advancing into the building, where I saw a dozen or more people moving about smartly, carrying files, boxes and sheaths of papers.

"How do you do?" I heard someone say, "I'm Whitehouse from Supply Services." It occurred to me that I had a slim chance of surviving without detection, perhaps for half an hour, if they were mostly strangers to one another – an ad hoc group assembled for the weekend before dispersal to their pigeon-holes in Whitehall. They wouldn't dream of intrusion. It must be a culture of complacency.

"Who are you?" This time, I realised the words were directed at me, by a big man with a sharp appraising gaze.

"I'm from Supply Services," I replied stiffly, in my best modulated pronunciation," with a slight nod towards my papers.

When the man gave me a casual thumb gesture to proceed, I realised that, so far, Polly's arrest had made no difference; no-one really believed in the possibility of a spy being at large, deep under the earth, with doors that rarely opened and a tunnel guarded by armed soldiers. I was someone that could not exist and therefore had freedom, for a short time, until they began to take stock of me and to ask questions.

I walked briskly down a corridor, past large offices, conference rooms and a staircase with signs pointing to guest suites, where I assumed important persons would have a style of accommodation more luxurious than that to which I was becoming accustomed. Just then, a small party came round the far corner of the corridor and I felt my heart beat fast when I saw the man I had nearly recognised on the station at Cheltenham. Now I was more sure of who he was. The strong, Jewish face was that of the man identified by Polly. It looked very much like Ben-Gurion, the chief architect of the state of Israel.

Before I could start serious speculation about the high drama in front of me, the group of about six men disappeared into a room, and so I carried on walking down the corridor until I came to an office in which women staff typed furiously or used duplicating machines as intently as a midwife awaiting a birth, except that their fingers were stained in ink instead of blood. I stepped inside and went calmly up to several piles of different documents, on one of which he read the heading, Conference: Project 101. I knew I had to act like an automaton, and so murmuring, "They want more of these," I picked up a paper from every pile and turned on my heel, while everyone else in the room looked on, not sure whether to shrug me off or to be astonished and alarmed.

Folding the papers and pushing them into the inside pocket of the jacket, I decided I had to gamble that they were worthwhile information and that I had to try to make my escape, since my enormous luck could only come before detection and capture. I imagined I could hear one of the women making a telephone call to the clerk who had distributed the documents: "Did you send someone to collect some

184

101 briefing papers? No? Well, someone has just been here..."

Sure that I could only retrace my steps, I coolly strolled back along the corridor and out of the building, where I saw several men in suits or in army uniform looking busy as they consulted lists or carried pieces of paper but actually doing nothing. I thought it was like being back in the Forces, and understood how Brummit could feel at home with the troglodyte life style. Then I became tense at the sight of the tunnel. There were no sentries standing there. It had only a black mouth in which the rail lines were swallowed up. I wondered if I could keep up my lackadaisical act, as I wandered closer to it.

"Hi you, that's off limits," someone yelled, but my blood was up and a sense of now or never drove me on into the blackness, running between the rails, panting with excitement. Then I felt a blow to my head, as I stumbled over a rail and into a wall. Pausing for a full minute, I felt a large bruise but was fit to continue, this time outside the track, with one hand feeling the wall. I wasn't sure if five or ten minutes had passed, when the sound of a train coming up behind me brought the sweat of fear to my face. It seemed logical, they'd run me down if they could, or jump out with flashlights to capture or kill me.

I saw it as desperate race to reach the faint haze of light that signified the end of the tunnel, before the train caught up with me. The noise resounded, but I gauged my pursuers were perhaps sixty yards away, when I felt buffeted by fresh air, as I came to the fading, early evening light. All I could do was to fling myself down the embankment and start to scramble through a hawthorn hedge, without heeding the scratches and pimples of blood on my hands and face, while hearing the train screeching to a halt. I stumbled up a sloping field, keeping close to the hedge. I had to rest. But that would mean surrendering to the men in khaki, who I imagined would any moment start to close in on me. They would be fresh after their ride on the train, whereas I felt an ache in every leg muscle. There was a pain across my chest as it pulsated in a hard effort to suck in the air.

I knew I was right about the determination of the hunters when I heard the crack of a rifle and a thudding sound evidently from the impact of a bullet, some distance away. It was like my own version of the Spanish Civil War! Someone was having target practice, but not at me. They are just scare tactics. That's a relief. But suppose they get serious. One bullet could finish me off.

A second shot landed near enough to spur me on through a gap in the hedge. Fear almost paralysed me, but next came a rush of hope when I saw a herd of cattle and a distant church spire, which had to mean I would soon see the imprint of another grey Cotswold village in a green hollow. I wondered if I would get to it I before I was caught, and what good it would do me if I did. They would still take me away and would surely have legal justification to arrest someone who had been prying in MOD offices.

Setting off at a desperate sprint in a half circle round the cows, I imagined the pain of a rifle shot into my shoulders. The animals stared at me accusingly, and then in two minds backed away a few steps. Once they were between me and the soldiers down the slope, I crouched low as I ran, hoping they screened me from anyone looking down a barrel, and glad that I was not as conspicuous as I would have been earlier. Then I heard the crash of bodies through the hedge, at a much lower point than where I had found the gap. Two men in khaki battledress and one in blue were perhaps a hundred and fifty yards away.

This was make or break. But they didn't appear to have rifles, probably because they would alarm and antagonise the village. I raced towards the steeple like a frightened hare, until a kissing gate delayed me. I ran another hundred yards alongside a brook and found myself in a churchyard, beyond which was a village street, with a car or two, a pub and a line of tidy, well maintained Cotswold cottages.

I staggered over flagstones, with a sense of defeat and conscious of my scratched cheeks and trousers daubed in cow dung. I heard a voice behind me say, with an Irish accent, "Don't be in too much of a hurry. I saw you running away from some men. Come in and have a cup of tea and rest up."

Spinning round I saw a pleasant-faced young man of about thirty, with a beard covering his jaw, and with a clerical collar. I knew I had no real choice but to accept the offer. There was no convenient bus about to depart or taxi at a stand. Capture was almost certain. At least I would have a witness of status, who would make it difficult for them to frogmarch me away.

I followed the priest into the vestry and said, "I'm not a criminal."

"OK. I'll buy that, for the time being. I don't know what the law would decide, but I regard you as being in sanctuary now. A few untruths on my part may not be sins, if I'm to give you a chance to convince me that you a good fellow. But I've got to get it right, as I'm not long ordained and here on approval."

I was wondering how much I should say, when I heard the sound of heavy footsteps approaching. The priest cautioned me to be silent and went outside to the footpath, leaving the door open, as though he had nothing to hide. I heard him say good morning, and then someone asked if he had seen a man run by, as he was wanted on criminal charges.

"Surely, I did," the priest said smoothly. "He has just gone up to the pub, though I saw a car just start up. Whether he got a lift, I can't say. I wasn't that interested."

There was more conversation that he couldn't hear and then a loud, "Thanks, vicar."

The priest returned to the vestry. "You aren't wholly safe here, despite what I said. It's a small church and anyone can poke his head anywhere. I can't keep anyone out. You'd better come over to my house. It would need a warrant for anyone to enter there."

I was led along a path through an orchard into the small, plainly furnished sitting room of a grey-stone house, where the first thing the priest did was to bring me bread, butter, cheese and a bottle of Guinness. As I spluttered my thanks, I was more nonplussed than I had been throughout my recent escapades. Why is this guy helping someone on the run? He's really cool and collected, and I'm completely dependent on him. It's scary.

As though reading my thoughts, the priest said, "You must be very surprised at this turn of events. I don't assist runaways every day of the week – in fact, I've never done it before, so I hope the Lord will forgive me, if He disapproves. But I'm on the side of the fox rather than the hunters and I place great importance on first impressions of people. You seem to be a sincere man. Tell me why you're on the run."

"I saw and heard things I shouldn't have."

"I see. Tell me a bit about yourself. I'm Paul Donovan, by the way. "

"My name is Joe."

I stood up and paced across the room, wondering how far I should unburden himself to this stranger. I felt I had nothing to lose and might gain a more balanced perspective on my troubles, which were coming in without pause, like a pile-up of debts.

"Sit down and talk as much or as little or as much as you wish," said the priest.

"There's not a lot wrong in being a political non-conformist. It's always seemed to me that the exercise of your beliefs is an essential part of living, not an optional extra. My father was an Irish nationalist and a friend of Michael Collins, so I'm not a conventional supporter of the political establishment, though I'm also not an advocate of violent measures to achieve a desirable end."

I sank into an armchair and said wearily, "Neither am I. I'm the victim of violence, not the perpetrator.

I was shot at when being chased, though I'm pretty sure the soldier deliberately missed and only intended to frighten me, so that I gave myself up."

My tongue was loosened. "Nothing seems to be going right for me. We live in a democracy, which is all very well, so long as you keep to norms of belief acceptable to those who hold power. If you don't, there's a big price to pay. I may lose my job."

The priest nodded his head vigorously before saying, "That figures. Slow down, though I can understand why you're agitated. Being shot at is frightening. I know because I was in the paras myself.

"No, don't tense up," he said, as I sat up straight with a look of alarm. "I was a Red Beret, but I'm also a Christian and can't deny the force of what you are saying. Whether it excuses your trespass is less clear. How did it come about?"

"That's a long story. Depends how far you want to go back. My parents were in the CP and I learned from them about the ruling class periodically leading us into war. I used to be a member myself but now have to decide whether I may achieve more if I join the party that gave us the NHS. More to the point, a friend who I work with at a college, told me about a secret rendezvous of ban-the-bomb people at this Ministry base, where important people would be taken when a nuclear attack was imminent."

"And did you think that by publicising these bases, they would become unusable and top people would have more of an incentive to avoid a war?" The priest queried me in a mild tone of voice, but looked at me intently.

"That might be true. I think we have a chance in this country to influence the big two Powers to enter serious nuclear disarmament talks if we lead the way. I can't see why a disarmed Britain would be a target."

"You may be right. I would put the emphasis on the immorality of preparations to kill tens of thousands of human beings. Perhaps the issue is facing the possibility of being invaded if we give up the bomb, or keeping it and therefore being prepared to use it. Incidentally, everyone round here knows about an underground warehouse where military stores are stockpiled. You seem to have found out it's more than that."

I told him where Polly and I worked, the events that had brought me to the churchyard, and everything I had seen and heard. "The most intriguing thing is the possibility of Ben-Gurion's presence in Gloucestershire. The Suez fiasco is over, so what's going on?

The priest shook his head. "Perhaps you mistook the man you saw. He may have been merely of the same physical type. Look at me. I'm of Irish extraction, with typical round, pale face and dark hair. You'd have difficulty in being sure it was me you were seeing, at a distance. By the way, I have a packet of Players. Do you smoke?"

"Not as a rule, but perhaps this once. Thank you."

We both lit up, and I continued. "There were several features of the face that were very individual, but there's no point in spending time on them now. My aim is to get back to my car and drive home, where I can take as long as is necessary to

191

telephone various newspapers. If they believed me and start their own investigations, it should help to get Polly freed, if she is still being held. We might both be able to go into work on Monday morning."

"I've got it!" the priest exclaimed. "Where is your car? I can get a friend to bring it here. My housekeeper is getting the last bus into Bourton shortly. I'll give her your keys, and you'll probably have your car here in an hour or so's time."

"I think I'd rather take a chance on the bus myself."

It seemed too much of a risk to let go of my keys. There could be a slip-up somewhere. What did I know about the housekeeper? And why had this man's tone become so insistent?

There was the sound of heavy boots outside, followed by a thunderous knock on the door. The priest stood up, but I rushed forward and barred his way to the door, saying, "You know who is outside, don't you? You asked them to give you twenty minutes with me, so you could hoodwink me, and discover everything I know about the base."

My frustration burst out in anger. "You're in so-called holy orders! You surprise me," I said, pushing the man hard with both hands, so that he fell over the sofa.

But the priest was on his feet again in a flash. "Keep your voice down. You're wrong about me, Joe. I'm capable of giving you a good scrap, if you insist on it. But I'm playing straight with you. It's a fact you can't go on avoiding the authorities, and you aren't the only judge of the national interest, but as far as I'm concerned, it's good luck to you for the time being. Now, out by the back door"

"Thanks. I'll see you again someday, if I'm not in prison."

Then I made a dash through the doorway into the kitchen, wrenched open the door into the back garden and ran through some woods, in which a bramble trailing across the path seemed suspicious, and the rustle of leaves as menacing as an ambush. I blundered into trees, which stood like sentries, but was thankful for the gathering dusk.

I assumed the pursuers must be close behind but felt disinclined to go into hiding, as they could take their time to comb the woods minutely. It was more likely they would set up a cordon of perhaps a mile radius and steadily close in, with every chance of netting me, unless I could cover much more ground before they could get me surrounded.

The woods petered out and were succeeded by a field of arable, with a hedge interrupted by a gate next to the road. I crouched at the edge of the gate, expecting to hear the noise of cruising vehicles, but there was no sound. Then I realised I had their tactics wrong. There would be no cowboys and Indians game in the fields. It would generate too much public interest and man-on-the-run publicity. They knew about the college. They would get my address, and find the car – they were probably looking for it now. If people enquired as to my whereabouts, the story could probably be I have had a mental breakdown, linked to the college enquiry into my behaviour, trouble with the police in London and other incidents, probably invented.

I mused over my new theory, which seemed so plausible that when I saw the pale lights of a vehicle approaching, pulling a trailer full of logs, I climbed over the gate, and waved for a lift. The driver let me into his muddy Land Rover, with a nod, in response to my question, "Bourton?" and we hardly exchanged a word for the next half-hour, as we lurched through narrow roads up to the outskirts of the village. I thanked the man and alighted two hundred yards from my car, which I had left in a residential street, rather than a car park.

The car still stood there, and sitting inside in the dark, with the occasional passer-by unaware of him, I relaxed for a minute with a fleeting sense of immunity from danger, but the feeling was followed by the desire to get out of the Cotswolds while the going appeared to be good. I had to find a safer place at once – but not before I had taken a quick look at document 101. Curiosity overcame caution.

CHAPTER 16

I switched on the pale, interior light and peered at my crumpled copy of Paper 101, headed Confidential Memo from the Foreign Offices of the UK and Israel. It referred to "a close political and military co-operation between our two nations.. . ...consolidated by a permanent alliance for peace and stability in the Middle East..."

   I thought the phrasing was a way of saying they had colluded in the Israeli attack on Egypt. The rest of the page just tried to show how the alliance fitted into the UN Charter. Well, I said to myself, that won't bring down the Government. It won't set Fleet St on fire. Wait a moment - this is more like it:

"Israeli Defence Ministry officials and Mr Ben-Gurion raised the nuclear issue at Sevres in September 1956 in their discussions with the French and British delegations about the Suez crisis. The question of supply of nuclear capability was agreed in principle by the French spokesmen, but reservations were expressed by the British Government.   Mr Ben-Gurion requested that a supply agreement be endorsed before military action at the end of October."

Reading it incredulously, I said aloud, "They've not only colluded in aggression – they're giving the atom bomb to Israel."

Soberly I wondered what I could achieve with the document. I didn't do so well in October, when I tried to tell the papers about the paratroopers. Most of them didn't want the Government to fall. Even the left-wing press might fight shy, when threatened with the Official Secrets Act, and half a dozen other statutes. There'd be only my word, and Polly's, against the MOD's.

Oh, hell - Polly! I haven't done a damn thing to help her. What can I do? Go to the police? What would they do? Hand them over to their friends who work for the MOD? It was trespassing on MOD property, after all. Best to get home and start to ring around.

I kept a careful watch in front and behind me, as I drove along an almost deserted road, past the glowing inns of Moreton in the Marsh, into Warwickshire and on to Birmingham. Countryside and town alike had a timeless air of relaxation inducing in me almost a mood of disbelief in the spectre of Suez or the nightmare of the atom bomb. What pantomime part was I playing? Perhaps I had some hallucinatory illness.

I approached my street warily, in the early hours, but heard no sound, as I parked by the rowan trees. Entering my apartment, I picked up the Saturday correspondence from the letter box, switched on the light, stood studying the envelopes and exclaimed out loud, "Home again! It's great to be back."

There was a voice, apparently from nowhere: "Seems you've had a busy day, Joe. Pity you didn't ask for permission, before you made yourself at home in other people's flats."

I looked up at a tall, sunburned man standing in the doorway between the room and the passage to my bedroom.

"Think a bit harder, Joe," the man said, with cool assurance. "You'll remember our brief meeting, that Saturday near the end of October. You came to London to hear the Welsh windbag in Trafalgar Square, and found yourself in a pub, where you started a brawl."

I recognised the military figure of my interrogator, who had buttonholed me, when I had been with Jacky. I shouted, "Who's the burglar now? Get out of my home!"

"It's a bit late to show concern for property rights, don't you think? You're an intruder and a thief. You stole food and clothes. You're being taken in for questioning."

"Not by you, or not till I've told a few night editors what I've seen today."

To my dismay, I saw over the man's shoulder two other figures in the passage. Realising that even a lucky throw that floored the policeman would be useless now, I bounded into the hallway, while feeling for my keys, opened the front door, shut it behind me and turned the key in the mortise, an instant before the Yale catch was opened from inside. After almost falling out of the building, I unlocked the car door and the warm engine started to a touch on the ignition. It had all happened so fast,

I found myself still clutching my letters, which I stuffed into a pocket.

I couldn't believe I'd managed it. It was only because that supercilious smarty had to stand preaching, instead of telling his men to grab me, as soon as I came in. They probably wouldn't jump out of a first-floor window, but they'll be after me soon. Where am I to go now? They'd have found out Polly's address. Tony is a possible help, but I'm not sure of him. Trevor might possibly take me in, but it wasn't likely and anyway what about his wife? There was always mother or Grandma but they'd trace them in no time. They had all the resources of the police, and I have nothing. These guys can force the door open and they'll also phone for help. Soon there'll be fast cars chasing me and I'll be done for, if I can't hide somewhere.

As I went down the list, I knew there was someone I could rely on, but she might not be alone and that would be embarrassing and galling, for myself, if not for Jenny. I drove very fast, instinctively along my usual route to college, with an idea in mind, remembering that the pavilion on the college's sports field had a window that could be prised open. It was really little more than a large shed, with two changing rooms, lavatories and hot and cold water for showers. If I could stay until dawn, I thought I might confuse my followers and then find a chance to make my telephone call, feeling thankful I still had my diary, in which I kept my telephone numbers.

After driving well inside the adjoining council estate, I left the car in a parking space, between a Zephyr and a Morris Minor, and walked quietly to the field's edge furthest from the college, which was a black cluster of buildings without a streak of moonlight crossing it. My arms trembling and aching, I pulled myself to the top of the wooden fence, dropped on to the grass and ran through the darkness to the changing rooms, where it took me only a short while to open the low window and clamber inside.

I curled up on a pile of old towels and sports kit and a feeling of despondency and failure overcame me, as I saw myself struggling against the odds. Did I want to show my devotion to Edward by following him into prison? I was fumbling with this thought when I fell asleep, exhaustion having overcome hunger and despair.

The sky was greying when I awoke, anxious, alert and cold, as I looked round my dismal surroundings, wondering if anyone might have left so much as a Mars bar, after Saturday's rugger match. I drank my fill of water from the sink and considered my options. I can't stay here. It'll be light soon. I'd better leave the car where it is. It could be a giveaway. Every policeman could be looking for a black Morris 8, with my registration.

I felt helpless and numb with indecision. I can be prosecuted for theft, if I give myself up. I would also be likely to lose my job. I have achieved nothing and could probably be ridiculed for being chased over the fields for trespass.

Then I grew angry at the thought of the big policeman, who had dogged me and was probably leading my pursuers. It would be good to give him one good punch in the face, even at the cost of being flattened by the man, who was probably skilled in unarmed as well as armed combat. More important, I still have the 101 card to play.

I looked in the mirror. Norton's suit was barely presentable. After washing myself and sponging my shoes and trousers with my handkerchief, I thought I might not attract curious glances in the street. It was hard to leave my austere refuge, but I climbed out of the window, retraced my steps and dragged myself over the fence, falling by force of gravity on to the pavement on the other side. I walked back through the council estate for about ten minutes, observing lamps without shades casting yellowish light on women in dressing gowns or slips and men putting on shirts over vests, until I reached the town, where I lingered in an alleyway for about half an hour, until I guessed some cafes would be opening, though I thought it too dangerous to go into one of them, even though I was ravenous. Now what? Perhaps I should try Tony first. It would be easier to ring Jenny from my place than from a public kiosk. I could go to Tony's by taxi but I ought to find out if it's safe. I think I'm all right for pennies.

I walked normally along the street, until I saw the red kiosk in the early morning light. I'd been to Tony's housewarming and the telephone number was in his diary. The dialling sound called a very long, insistent challenge but the receiver was eventually picked up. It was Tony, who answered tensely, "I have already had some visitors," and put the phone down.

I felt anger at the curt statement, but then it occurred to me that Tony might have been breaking off the call before the kiosk could be traced by anyone tapping the phone line. Reading a warning to get out of the area, I ran hard along the pavement, turning corners and crossing to the other side of streets, until I thought it best to slow down, in case my heaving chest drew looks from passers-by, who were now a steady flow. Perhaps it was like a fox felt. I'd got to go to ground. But where? I know where. Thank goodness my diary with the address was in my pocket. I could make it before she went out. A number 13 bus would do it. There was one coming....upstairs would do me... it was only a three-penny ticket to the terminus.

I well knew the area, which was full of Victorian terraced houses, with up and down bay windows framed by thick, white pillars. Many were split into flats and after looking in the diary again I found the house and rang a bell. I heard a light, rapid footfall coming down stairs, and when the door was opened looked at the face of my student, Lin, wide-eyed with surprise. "May I come in? I need help," I said without ceremony, in a tone of urgency.

"Yes, of course," she replied, with a note of apprehension in her voice, as she pulled her kimono more closely to her chest. "You look terribly white and tired. Come in and sit down."

I followed her up to the top floor into a sitting room, which was tidy, sparsely furnished, with books piled on the floor, beside a large, full bookcase. Chinese woven pictures on the walls were its only ethnic identity.

I heard myself talking in a hoarse, nervous manner, with no trace of the assured and slightly pompous lecturer that she had known. "I'm thankful you gave me your address, and hope you won't be sorry you did. I'm wanted by the police for entering and spying on a secret underground base, which I believe is ready as a home for Government ministers, civil servants and other chosen people, in the event of a nuclear war. I've also discovered some political secrets, which would be very damaging to the Government, if made public. Can I stay here for a few hours and make some phone calls, particularly to a friend who will help me?"

"I trust you, Mr Butler. It was lucky we had that discussion in college. We got to know each other well enough for me to agree to help you, if you are in political trouble, and you can use the telephone, of course."

I heard the dialling sound on Jenny's phone, my impatience and despair increasing as it became clear that no one was there. My cheeks wet with a tear, I turned to Lin and said, "I'm sorry, I don't mean to be a nuisance. Can I try later?"

She put a hand on my shoulder and said, "It is an honour to help you. You can stay with me as long as you wish. I will get you some breakfast. It is Sunday morning and so I am in no hurry to go anywhere."

"Thank you," I said. I felt relaxed by her compassion, and when she came in with some cornflakes, toast and coffee, a feeling of gratitude swept over me. I saw she had on a blouse and slacks, and was wearing lipstick. She was very attractive. It would be a good place to stay for a while. I called myself a damn fool. I had to grow up, instead of thinking like a Pinkerton, eyeing up a Butterfly. It was time to show some responsibility.

I said, "You're a lovely person, and I should like to become a friend, and in some way to repay your kindness to me."

She said, "I think we are already good friends. You were upset just now. Tell me, were you telephoning someone who is more than a friend to you?"

"Yes and no. We were very close for a short while, but we had to part, and I think she has found someone else. But she would help me, if she knew I was in trouble."

"I hope you come together again, as I believe you would really like it to happen."

"I don't think that can ever happen. But I'm too concerned about myself. Polly Kaufmann, the Politics lecturer, was with me in the underground base yesterday. She was arrested and may be in serious trouble. If they let her go, she may be back at home. It isn't safe to telephone her. The line will be tapped."

"I know her. She is very friendly with overseas students. She told me once that her parents were immigrants. I can go to her house now, quite easily, on my bicycle."

"Well, be careful. I have her address. All you need say is that I wanted to know if she was all right. If you see a car outside or anyone standing nearby, show no interest, but cycle past and come back here. While you're away, if you agree, I'll try one or two calls, although on Sunday, the people I want to talk to at one or two newspaper offices are unlikely to go in to work until the afternoon. I have a two or three-hour wait. You'll be back much sooner than that."

As soon as she left the flat, I rang Directory Enquiries and found the numbers of the Daily Worker and the Manchester Guardian. There was no one to answer the phone at the Worker, but the Guardian had a man on duty. He was alert but sceptical:

"You say you have seen an underground base, and Ben-Gurion or his look-alike was there. How can you be sure of that? Have you met Ben-Gurion? You say you have another witness. Where is she? You don't know? Look, the best thing you can do is to come down here to talk to us, face to face. I'm saying this to you, because nine times out of ten, callers don't turn up when invited, and our time isn't wasted. It's up to you. Good day."

I knew I would have to go to Manchester or London straightaway, or as soon as I felt it was safe. Stationing myself by the window, I peered out between a curtain and the wall. My vigil had lasted for half an hour, when a black car pulled up on the other side of the road and I saw four men in suits get out and walk smartly in my direction. Like a startled wild animal I rushed to the door, paused and then bounded up some stairs to an attic. Seeing a sloping ceiling with a skylight half pushed open, I ran to it and pushed the ratchet handle to its fullest extent, so that there was a two and a half foot square gap, through which I could pass without great difficulty.

The thought of clinging to the roof made me shiver with fear, but a sense of inevitability and fatalism filled my mind. I knew I had to do it. There

204

was no other way out, unless I surrendered. The ceiling slanted at a forty-five rather than sixty-degree angle. That was good, as I could lean a little on the roof, though it was made of slates, which would give poor purchase to my fingers. My head spun at the vision of myself losing my grip and falling and crashing onto the yard of the three-storey house. I told myself it was too stupid and akin to madness, while knowing that a driving force was over-riding the instinct of self-preservation.

I pulled a chest of drawers over to the window and stood on top, head bent and shoulders up against the sloping ceiling, so that I could pull my head and chest through the window frame. I then leant on the frame, brought up one leg and thrust it outside, while pivoting my weight on my hands and turning my upper body back into the room. Holding the frame I let both feet slide over the slates until they reached the gutter, I dare not entrust with my full weight. My heart was thumping like a hammer but my head stayed cool. As I prepared to move crablike across the slope of the roof, I knew I must never look down but keep one foot in the gutter to guide and stabilise me.

It seemed an age before I dared to let go of the window frame and cling only to the overlapping edges of slates, thankful that the roof was not even five degrees steeper. After a foot or two's nervous advance, I thought that the stiffness in my arms and legs would force me to let go and put my weight on the gutter, which would surely give way, so that I slid off the roof to my death in the yard below. It flashed through my mind that it would be damn convenient for Mr Sunburn, who could just leave my body and go home. I would be a heap of refuse by the dustbins.

The idea of an ignominious end to my drama switched on a rush of adrenaline, and digging my fingers into slight gaps between some of the slates I speeded up my progress, until I grasped the line of bricks dividing the house from the next one in the terrace.

The relief did not last, for as soon as I looked at my next objective, a similar, open skylight next door, the tension gave me cramp in one leg, and my feeling became one of helplessness, almost apathy towards my fate. The urge to look down became almost irresistible, until a banging that sounded like forced entry to the house broke the spell. I resumed my crawl across the second roof, inspired by the sight of an open window. I reached it, and sobbed for a minute, looking at my blackened, bleeding fingers and torn nails. I thrust one wrist over the ledge, and then the other, and with a final, unremitting act of will forced my arms and shoulders up, under the window, which was open about a foot. The ledge took my body's weight and I edged forward until I fell hands first to the floor of the room, where I lay panting and dizzy, as though I had finished a Marathon run.

I wanted to go on lying there, despite a background noise, but the desire for safety cleared my head and I realised there was a loud orchestral sound coming from nearby. I got to my feet, feeling weak in every muscle and shivering. Holding onto the window frame, I looked at the room's junk and when I was ready trod around old bedsteads, mattresses, boxes of books and coat hangers towards the door. I thought it might be Schubert's Great Symphony that I heard, and after tip-toeing along a carpeted hallway, I glanced very carefully into a room, the door of which was open about six inches. I saw an elderly woman hunched in bed, beside which stood a record player in an oak cabinet. Luck's on my side. I think it's the Fifth Symphony. Anyway, she can't hear me and won't easily be disturbed by the noise next door.

I made my way downstairs, and was relieved not to hear a sound on the other two floors, apart from the music from upstairs. Advancing cautiously to the kitchen, I looked out at an untidy vegetable garden surrounded by a yew hedge high enough to hide him from someone standing outside next door. Opening the door slowly I stepped out, glanced around and ran silently to the bottom of the garden, where a gate opened into an alley running between two lines of gardens. I sprinted to the far end, where I was at once on a busy street. I knew I must look like a bedraggled, dirty-faced drunk who had slept all night in a hedgerow, but I steeled myself to get on a bus going towards the centre of town. On the top deck there were two other people, who showed interest only in each other.

I suddenly felt relaxed, light-headed and optimistic. I've made it. I've enough cash to get to London, where I'll go the round of the newspapers to see what interest there is in my story. All I have to do is keep on to the terminus and get the next coach out. Once it all goes public, I may even go back to work tomorrow. Five minutes of fame should keep me safe from prosecution, and Polly will have to be freed, if she's still being detained.

As the bus drew in to the terminal driveway, I looked out at several children whirling their hula-hoops, as they waited with their parents for a bus to take them out to the country park, which was crowded with factory workers and their families on Sundays. I should like to be on a day out, with a child or two, and, of course, a wife. But who could I marry?

When the bus stopped, I ran downstairs, almost into the arms of a man in a raincoat, and a spasm of fear gripped me. It was all up. They had traced my movements, or guessed I would take a bus to the centre. I breathed hard, prepared to make a dash for it, but the man said, "Sorry, no harm done, I trust," smiled and turned towards the lower deck. I couldn't stop myself laughing hysterically, until I saw I was attracting more attention to myself than I had done all morning.

"No problem at all," I said. "It was my fault. I'm in too much hurry to meet my girl.

CHAPTER 17

I was sure mother would be angry and very upset, when the police went round. I had to get in touch to tell her I was all right. Hurrying inside a newsagent's shop, I bought some stationery and resting the paper on a shelf wrote to say that I was safe and sound, but could not visit her, owing to pressing circumstances that I would fully explain later. The shop sold stamps, and there was a post-box in the same street. Further along there was even a café, where I almost gave way to the temptation to have a cup of tea. I thought I could sit on a bench at the back of the warm, muggy room, shielded from the street by a group of postmen standing with mugs and bacon butties in their hands. But I couldn't be sure – postmen were observant people. The police might have shown them my photo.

I thought gloomily of how my problems at work could spiral out of control, once Jones knew of my plight. He would obviously be told. He'd pass it on, unless they told him to keep it secret. They might do that, if they thought they could silence me. A hush, hush policy would suit them best. The question was how they intended to keep me quiet. I had five pounds. It would get me to London, but the station would be watched. I needed a place where I could think through my course of action. There was one possibility, though how safe was it? Special Branch would know of Grandma's house.

I took a taxi to the house with the faded stucco, where there was no guard on the door or car parked on the roadway. A middle-aged woman wearing a large white apron opened the door and said she was sent every day by Social Services. I looked at her carefully but told myself not to be so suspicious, as paranoia was more hindrance than help. I entered Grandma's room and thought she looked even more shrunken than ever. A fleeting image of a body in the orange box came to mind.

"Gran,"I said, "there's something I must tell you. I'm on the run from Special Branch or MI5, or whatever they're called. I've found out things they don't want me to know."

She looked at me, wide-eyed. "You're a chip off the old block, if ever there was one. Edward was innocent of wrongdoing, but they came after him and sent him to prison. All he did was to lead a demonstration of the unemployed. I was in the crowd outside the prison, shouting, "Free Edward Butler!"

As I heard her quavering tone, I felt guilty for burdening her with my problems, but she became more spirited, and half raised herself from her chair, as she added: "Stay here as long as you need to. No one's been around. It's a safe place. No one will think that I'm capable of any law breaking. I'm almost ninety."

"Thanks, Gran. I'll see how it goes. It would be useful to stay overnight and get a decent sleep."
"Well then. Take this."

She reached down beneath the cushion of her chair to the lining and pulled out an envelope. She took out six five-pound notes and offered them to him. "I've nothing to spend it on, except my funeral, and I've enough left for that."

I knew I could not refuse the money, if I wanted to go to London. "Gran," I said, "it's just what I need. I can't go to the bank. I shall pay you back very soon, I'm sure."

After pressing my lips to her forehead, I sat with her for a few minutes, until the carer beckoned me into the kitchen and told him the old lady would soon have to go into hospital, for investigation of pains in her chest. "There's no immediate cause for alarm, though she can't live alone much longer."

I imagined the lump on grandma's back growing bigger and draining her strength, while she remained fully aware of her body's humiliation, without the quick release that a coronary had given Granddad.

"You look famished," she said, when I re-entered her room. "Have some bacon and eggs." I went into the kitchen to cook them myself, after foraging in the pantry. My mouth began to water and I felt almost cheerful, until the low voice of the carer in the hallway made me tense.

I crept to the half open door and saw her speaking into the telephone. I heard the words, "He's been here for about twenty minutes." I darted into the living room, to give Grandma a quick kiss, before going out through the front doorway.

"You lousy informer!" I said quietly, so as not to alarm Grandma. Brushing past her as she shrank against the wall, I ran down the garden path.

I strode rapidly through the back roads, thinking it would be policy to catch a bus to the railway station at a stop away from the main road. I was sure I was risking almost inevitable arrest. Every policeman on the beat would be on the look-out for me, probably with a copy of the picture that was in my flat, showing me standing alongside mother. I wished I could see her. Why shouldn't I go straightaway? I'd been to Grandma's. At least, I could take a look. It should be possible for me to see if the house was being watched.

Stopping at the first kiosk I came across, I phoned for a taxi, which set off at speed towards mother's house, except that it took an unusual route. I said to the driver, a silent, middle-aged man, "Why are you going by Broad Avenue? Are you trying to lengthen the journey?"

"No, mate. Just taking you by the way I know best."

I knew my suspicion was almost certainly a fantasy, but when we stopped at some traffic lights, I jumped from the taxi, after throwing a shilling down on the floor of the cab. There was no help for it. There was no time to see mother. I had to go to London to the newspaper offices. They'd have people there on Sunday afternoon.

It seemed a good idea to avoid Birmingham New St Station by travelling from Wolverhampton, and another taxi took me there. The railway seemed asleep, with not a porter or a policeman or a soldier with a kit-bag in the entrance hall or on the iron steps leading up to the black bridge spanning the platforms. I examined the timetables and saw there was a London train in an hour's time. May as well get my ticket now. Then I could find a teashop somewhere in the centre and come back to get on board as quick as possible, to try to avoid being seen.

There was no trouble with the ticket, as I handed over one of grandma's five pound notes. As waited for the change, I imagined the door beside me opening, and then two large men coming out and grabbing my arms, with perhaps a voice saying, in a familiar, arrogant tone: "Hullo, smart-arse. You know the saying, 'All things come to those who wait.' Well, we waited, and you came."

But nothing happened, and I decided that in real life the hunters were not as super-efficient in pursuit of their quarry as they were in spy films. I still dodged back inside the entrance to the station when a police car appeared from nowhere. This was it. Which way could I run? No way, except along the track and into the tunnel. Then a young woman alighted from the car after kissing one of the officers on the cheek and calling back, "Goodbye, daddy," before walking to the steps leading to a bridge across the line to the Liverpool train.

The officers hung around instead of driving off, and once more I was on my guard. They could still be keeping the place under observation, and that seemed more than possible when they got out of the car and entered the ticket office. Taking my chance, I ran lightly from the station and down a side alley, into a mean street. I walked through the litter of fish and chip wrappers, and past grubby shop windows filled with miscellaneous cheap new or second-hand goods, whether old measuring balances and door locks, packets of sherbet, with straws, or bags of flour that looked like government surplus from some past war. It had the look of an unreconstructed street from the thirties or even twenties. Kids in worn jackets and their older brothers' short trousers reaching well below their knees still sat on the steps of a Mitchell and Butler's pub, and I thought of the elder brothers who had sat there before them, in the same clothes. A large pile of coke stood outside a terraced house with yellowing net curtains, and I wondered how long it had been there and when the occupants would shovel it through into their back yard.

The men and women were short and wiry or short and stout, like workers in the iron and steel and mining industries, or else their descendants. Their conversational tones in the pub ran musically up and down the scale but were contorted by the Black Country accent, which was no worse, I told myself, than the strangulated Cockney sound I had heard on stage from Eliza Doolittle. I remembered warmly a time when my car had broken down in West Bromwich High Street. Men like these had swarmed round it, got their hands greasy from the engine and helped me on my way, with a "That's all right, mate." These old communities had a social solidarity, unlike the more recent and better-off towns, where they'd be more likely to leave you to fend for yourself.

"'Ave yo 'ad a fall, mate?" asked a rotund, red-faced middle-aged man with long, grey hair.

"Aye," I replied. "I slipped on the grass, this morning."

"Well, our kid, if I was you, I'd look out. Plain-clothes police come in here, showing around pictures of faces they want to meet up with."

I felt my cheeks flush. "Thanks," I said softly.

The other man laughed loudly. "Not much need to keep your voice down, our kid. The people in this pub aren't likely to split on you. They don't like coppers enough for that. What you been up to?"

"I saw and heard things I shouldn't have seen in a Government underground warehouse in the country."

"Is that all? I do worse things every day. What was in the warehouse? Tanks and guns and uniforms? Anything saleable?"

"Not really. It was more a hideaway for the Government, if there is an atomic war."

"Oh, I see. A safe place for V.I.Ps. Definitely not for the likes of us. Tell you what, kid. I don't mind fixing you up for a few days. You can kip down in the hut and I'll pay you by results, if you give me a hand on loading up. What do you say?"

I looked hard at him, and he seemed sincere enough. "All right, that would certainly suit me. Thank you very much."

"Well then. I said the folks in this pub don't snitch to the cops. But I can't vouch for everybody. There's one or two who might see a way of getting off charges if they informed on you. So I'll go out now and you take another twenty minutes – have a pint –

before you get up and go. I'll be at the far end of the street, after I've looked in to see one of my daughters. My name's Reuben, by the way."

"And I'm Joe."

Reuben loudly wished me farewell and without looking back strolled out of the pub, after exchanging words with people he knew. I had a pint of mild, but there was no cheese batch on sale and I felt very hungry when after making a leisurely exit I walked rapidly along the street, hardly expecting to see my benefactor again. But Reuben was there and led the way through alleyways and streets into an area where the buildings were all very old and some had corrugated iron walls and roofs, like a picture of a South African shanty town. He took a large key to a monstrous padlock on pock-marked wooden double doors, and when these swung open I saw a surprisingly large cavern, almost filled with scrap metal in all sorts of forms, from car engine blocks to gas cookers and mounds of lead piping.

"I need this shifting as soon as possible. You'll be working with our Artie. His workmate's in dock after coming off his motorbike and breaking a leg. Come in here and see where you'll be sleeping."

I was taken into a small room partitioned off from the rest of the warehouse and containing some chairs, a desk littered with what looked like invoices, and a bed along one wall.

"You haven't got nice sheets and blankets but it'll keep you warm," Reuben said apologetically, pointing to a pile of old counterpanes, and a cushion that evidently served as pillow. "But there's summat else I want to speak to you about."

They sat down on the chairs and Reuben looked seriously at me, before saying, "Are you a political activist?"

"You might say so, up to a point, but nothing like my parents were." I wondered where the question was leading, and whether the older man was in with the police, after all.

"I worked in a munitions factory in the war and helped to sell lot of pamphlets and collected thousands of pounds for the Red Army. It wasn't half a busy time. Especially for me, when my wife ran off with a soldier. I followed them and gave him one punch. 'Keep her,' I says, and I meant it. Then I went home to look after our Artie – you'll meet him soon.

"After the war I went into the scrap metal business and had no time for politics, but I haven't changed my views. One day, if they get the chance, this lot will lead us into a war against Russia."

"Perhaps they will, if the Yanks lead the way. They'll soon repair the American alliance, on any terms. Then they'll both rule the Middle East, with then Yanks top dogs. If Eden can stand up in the House of Commons and deny there was a secret agreement for Israel to start the war against Egypt, there's nothing they won't do, in the name of the national interest."

Reuben wanted to know more about Israel and the war, saying, "It might be all about empire-building and the interests of the big capitalist companies. I dunno. What gets me is the secrecy and cover-ups."

I talked politics but it would be premature to tell him everything about what I had seen in the nuclear shelter. Better to get the whole story in a newspaper, before it began to leak out and become distorted.

I changed the subject and questioned Reuben about how he had found his feet after the war. I was always interested to see how the war workers had adapted to peacetime conditions. One of Edward's soul mates in the factory was now a successful bookmaker. Reuben might grow rich in the scrap business. It was a strange turnaround – socialists and communists becoming capitalists. How long would it take before some of them changed their politics and became Tories?

My new friend took my arm, saying, "You can have some nosh with me, by the way, as I only live next door."

I wondered why I was not invited to sleep there, but the reason became obvious, when I entered Reuben's living quarters and found I had to climb over cardboard boxes of lampshades, electric kettles, cosmetics, shoes and other stock.

"Monday to Friday is scrap metal," Reuben explained, "but Artie and me takes this stuff down the market on Saturdays. So there ain't a lot room in the house. The two of us live here on our own. As I told you, my missus left when he was a nipper. By the way, we have corn' beef sandwiches for dinner and usually stew at night. I hope it suits you."

"It'll be like dining at the Ritz."

Just then, Artie, a blond, taciturn young man with his father's sturdy build, drove up in a lorry, and I turned to with relish, helping to load it with lead piping and some cookers, ready for delivery under a deal Artie had made on the other side of town.

An idea came to me. "I'll come with you to give you a hand unloading," I said, seeing a chance to telephone my mother, well away from where I would be lying low with Reuben. It might put the police off the scent, if they were tapping his mother's telephone line.

We set off, with Artie crooning *Peggy Sue* throughout the quarter of an hour's ride to another warehouse, where in exchange for the stuff he pocketed a bundle of pound notes, with no receipt, just a "Thanks, mate." On the way home Artie stopped at a phone booth and I made my call, with a fast-beating heart, thinking if they'd been round to interrogate her, she'd be frightened, not for herself but for me.

A nervous "Yes?" answered my call, but when I spoke, she poured out a torrent of emotion. "Where are you, Joe – don't tell me, there'll be somebody listening in. Are you all right? What have you been doing? They came round and said that a friend had reported that you were missing, but they wouldn't tell me the name of the friend. I didn't trust them. I remembered when Edward's bicycle crossbar was three-parts cut through, soon after he was being followed by a man from the C.I.D. What have they done to you?"

"I'm fine, mom. I'm on the police wanted list, because I saw some things they want to be kept secret. I think I'm in the right. I used to think there was nothing much left to fight for. But I was wrong.

It's no different, except that people are better off. I feel a bit like you and Edward, twenty, twenty-five years ago."

"It's lovely just to hear you. I wish I could see you, but that's impossible, so long as you want to keep clear of the police."

"I've been to see grandma briefly. She's very low most of the time."

Dorothy replied with some tension in her tone: "I've been thinking about her a lot recently. It may be the time for me to put a proposition to her that not long ago she would have rejected outright. I'll go to see her. At this moment I'm more anxious about you. What are you going to do?"

"I'm trying to work things out. I'll give you another call in two or three days' time, but I'd better put the phone down now, in case it's being traced to this call box. Bye for now."

For the next two days, I loaded scrap onto the lorry, or new supplies from the lorry into the storehouse, and found that the lifting became easier with practice. Artie helped me with most of the cookers, and I was pleased to find an easy relationship begin to grow up between us. Artie's leisure interest was greyhound racing, and he tried to persuade me to accompany him to an evening meeting.

"I've got a system, Joe. You can't lose. You back the traps, not the dogs. Put your money on the first trap that has two winning dogs. The odds are it'll have a third."

"How many thousands have you won, with this system?"

"Well, to tell the truth, I've not yet tried it. I've just backed what I fancied. But now I'm going to be more scientific."

"Best of luck. I'd love to come with you, but there'll be policemen there, and they've probably got my picture. It wouldn't be a good idea."

"Okay. Another time, perhaps. How long are you going to be on the run? All your life?"

"I hope not," I said, but I had asked myself the same question many times, and the following morning, at the corned-beef break, thought about my next move. I could make a dash for London. Reuben's two fivers would help and I could afford a taxi or a private hire car all the way or risk going by train. I couldn't stay put much longer, as the question of keeping my job at Midland Central faced me with increasing urgency.

As Reuben sat down, he said, "Where's Artie got to?"

His son answered for himself as he ran into the storehouse at full speed. "It's the cops," he panted. "Their car is at the end of the alley, and they're coming this way."

I sprang up. I'll race them," I said.

Reuben shook his head. "You'll never do it. They'll have men at both ends of the street. That's the way they catch the bookie's runners. Someone in the pub must have snitched. There's only one thing for it. Get in there, Joe." He pointed to one of many large packing cases, with their lids off, and partly filled with straw. They had contained government surplus crockery that he said was well worth his while to sell to market stallholders.

I crouched inside the case, and was covered lightly by straw, which I partly pushed aside so that I could breathe easily. Then I was lifted and moved several yards, and heard other cases being moved near to me. Reuben and Artie seemed to settle down, and I heard Reuben's instructions:

"Make sure all the boxes with straw look as though they have about the same amount....And take Joe's sandwich....Now relax. We won't deny he's working for us. I'll say he's gone to the shops."

I thought it might be a false alarm, but ten minutes later heard the sound of men's feet, and a conversation went as Reuben had expected.

"Course I know Joe. I met him in the pub, as you probably know. He said he could do with some temporary work, and so I took him on. He's a strong lad, doing a good job, helping me out, while one of my workers is on the box. Why? What's up?"

"We want to ask him some questions. How long's he been gone?"

"Only a few minutes."

"All right. Mind if we have a look round – here and in your house?"

"Not at all. Help yourself. Mind you, if he has a guilty secret, he'll probably run a mile if he sees you hanging around."

I heard someone walking round the boxes, but the policeman was not interested enough to bother to turn over the straw. Then the sound of the men's feet died away.

"They'll be in their cars, keeping watch at both ends," said Artie, in a burst of eloquence.

"They'll be back to make a full search, when Joe doesn't appear," said Reuben. "I tell you what I'll do. Harold, next door but one, is an old mate, who'll take you in, and when it's dark, we'll get you away somewhere safe. I'll just go out the back and call him."

I decided I wouldn't put Reuben to any more trouble after today, but was glad to be led out and over two fences into the house of Harold, a gaunt, white-haired former steelworker, who gripped me with enormous hands and sat me down in his own armchair. "They'll never get into here without a warrant," he said vehemently. "Let's have a cup of tea."

He spent the next two hours explaining to me how the molten iron was cast, and how he used to sweat and drink five pints of Ansells mild every morning to quell his thirst. Late in the afternoon, cars pulled up in the street and police swarmed over Reuben's store and also searched his home, as he had forecast. No-one troubled Harold, but when it was dark Reuben crossed over to the back door, and said that they should go, as Artie had scouted the area and found no sign of a policeman or a car with anyone sitting inside.

"I shall never forget what you've done for me," I said, "but enough is enough. I'm going to London by taxi. I don't trust the railway stations."

"All right. We'll go a roundabout way out of this area."

223

I followed him along alleyways at the back of the houses into a parallel main street, where Reuben rang round and found a private hire car driver who was willing to go to London for twenty pounds paid in advance. I felt it was my best course of action, even though it was possible that the driver would betray me to the police.

"Thanks a million, Reuben. I shall keep in touch with you when all this is over."

Then I sank into a back seat for the trip south.

CHAPTER 18

I felt like an actor in the footlights, as the oncoming traffic lit up my face. I had the lead part. I thought excitedly of the press publicity that would explode when I told the story of the Anglo-French plot to give Israel her reward for aggression against Egypt. How many Israelis knew that their Government had decided to equip themselves with weapons that could threaten a new Holocaust for their Arab neighbours? I was about to expose the whole rotten business.

When we reached outer London, the driver stopped at the kerb and turned round to face me. I recognise your face, you know. The police circulated your picture to all the taxi and private hire firms. But I'll give you a chance. I've seen a few criminals in the back of my car, and you ain't one of 'em. I want another five pounds for taking you to your destination and then keeping my mouth shut. Fair enough?"

"Fair enough," I said, almost laughing with relief. "Take me south of the river."

The Daily Worker was housed in a building so secure that I feared I would never make any one answer the door. Eventually, an elderly lady opened a shutter and eyed me suspiciously. "What do you want at this time of night?" she asked.

"I've an urgent news story," he said. "It's about Israel and the atom bomb."

"Oh, all right. Wait a minute and I'll make some enquiries."

A quarter of an hour later, the door was opened, and I entered a dingy passageway, from where I was led into a small room, where a gaunt young man introduced himself edgily as the duty sub-editor. "I can't spare more than five minutes at the outside. Work's mounting up and I shall drown in paper if I don't go back soon to bail most of it into the waste bins. Are you the man who was reported missing by the Mirror, after discovering some government underground store place in Gloucester?"

"Yes, I am. But there's a lot more to it than that discovery. First, the so-called warehouse has dozens of flats ready for occupation in the event of a war. Needless to say, you and I won't be invited to take a break there. Secondly, I saw someone who was very likely Ben-Gurion, attending hush-hush talks about transfer of nuclear bomb secrets to Israel."

"Really?" The young man's interest seemed to have more than a touch of scepticism. "Did you have anyone else with you at the time?"

"Yes, there was a work colleague, a woman whose whereabouts I am not sure of at present. She may be free, but she could be imprisoned. I've been on the run and even shot at."

"Are you sure about all this? The first thing I must have is a statement from the other witness. I need to see her."

"Well, look at this document."

As I showed the man his copy of Paper 101, I felt the deflation of his initial enthusiasm. Without Polly to support me, my evidence was shaky. It could be dismissed as the words of someone who was off their trolley.

"How did you get this letter?" said the young man, after reading it carefully, with furrowed brow."

"I took it by false pretences. Does it matter?"

"I'm afraid it does. If this document was stolen or obtained by false pretences, you could go to jail for two years under the Official Secrets Act, and so could the editor of this paper. Or we might be fined a sum that would ruin us. The best thing you could do, would be to circulate it as a leaflet, so that it gets into the public domain. Then the papers may be prepared to report it, after consultation with their lawyers. A further problem is that it isn't signed. That reduces it significance. You could have written it yourself."

"So that's the reality of freedom of speech – so unlike the gagging of the press in Russia."

"Yes, that's about it. Where the interests of the state are concerned, the iron fist emerges from the velvet glove."

"Thanks, and goodnight."

The London office of the Manchester Guardian received me courteously, but this time, a young man with an Oxbridge air of assurance put the message more bluntly. "You admit you pinched this paper from an office of the Ministry of Defence. It doesn't matter whether the office was underground or on a mountain top. The police are pursuing a common thief. I should do my duty and telephone them that you are here. But of course, I won't, because I'm a journalist, interested in your story, but aware that it needs corroboration. Can you find the girl who was with you? We might take a chance on publication, if two people were eyewitnesses to a supposed Ben-Gurion sighting. You must realise it would be strongly denied and attempts would be made to make you out as a sensation-seeking fool, who in his eagerness for publicity mistook one face with Jewish features for another, more famous one."

I thanked the man and after promising to phone in the next day, left the office to find a quiet pub where I could think about my next move. It looked as though my story was not as compelling as I had hoped. I had hardly been hailed as a hero, and there would be no picture of me on any front page. I walked along the pavement slowly, almost into the arms of two policemen turning into my path from another street.

"Sorry, sir," one of them said. "All right then, no reason to back away like that. It was an accidental collision. We aren't out to get you."

"Hang on, Bill," the other one said. There may be a reason for the gentleman's anxiety. I think I've seen his face before."

He grabbed one of my arms, and the other officer took hold of the other one. One of them summoned a car by radio, and I was thrust on to the back seat, in between the two impassive men who held him. I fantasised for a moment or two about a dramatic bid to escape, but one look at his guards convinced me that the likely result would be a knockout blow to my jaw or solar plexus. I let my body grow slack, as we were edged through the traffic between the towering buildings of central London, until the car turned into a yard somewhere off Whitehall. I've had it now. It's all over. They've completely got the better of me. The hyenas have won.

I was led through the windowless corridors that I had dreamed about, and down flights of steps to a cell, where I was deposited by two men in dark blue uniform, and locked up. The walls and ceiling were brown as earth. I thought of a grave in a field. Later, I was given, to my half-amusement as I thought of Reuben, a corned beef sandwich and a mug of tea. I would have given Norton's suit in exchange for a newspaper or a book, but the room was empty, except for a mattress and blanket on the floor, a washbasin, a large bucket with a lid, and a toilet roll nearby

There followed a long evening and a night in which I lay awake for some time, thinking of my helplessness, but also of possible rejoinders to the questions that were obviously going to come my way. I decided I would say nothing but simply insist on having a solicitor present. Dammit, I .they're parties to a conspiracy to deceive the public. If I'd been able to avoid arrest, the sordid story might have been public knowledge by now.

Later on, my belief that an orderly process of law might resolve my predicament seemed so much self-delusion. It all might have been so different. My adventures would have seemed heroic if the newspapers had published my story. Nobody outside MI5 and Special Branch even knew where I was, not even Jenny.

Anyway, my love for her was hopeless. My relationships had always unravelled. I was an oarsman whose boat was drawn into the rapids. It was 1957 and life was getting better for most people, but not for me, Joe Butler. I was only 28, with nothing to look forward to. I had snatches of sleep and then stared up at the high panes letting in the grey, early light that cast shadows of the iron bars onto the opposite wall.

It was still early morning when the same two men who had brought me into the cell came back, accompanied by my old acquaintance the sunburned man, who stepped forward to ask the questions.

"Well, look who I have here. It's the clever bugger who was fighting in the pub. I warned you where we'd take you, if we had to, and here's where you've ended up. We're not messing about any longer. We know you are a ban-the-bomb person who set out on Saturday morning to gain illegal entrance to a government storage base in the Cotswolds. You stole papers and the suit you are wearing. Is there any reason why you shouldn't be taken to court for trespass and theft?"

"I suppose there must be – otherwise you'd do it. You don't want the publicity."

"Don't be impertinent, you sod," the other man said. "Just answer the question plainly, with no cheek. Understand?"

I nodded, with a sense of defeat. I couldn't do a thing. This man with the two other officers would massacre me. if I tried anything. .

Very well," my questioner continued. "Tell me exactly what you saw inside the storage area."

"I saw the flats, and the railway line, and military personnel."

"What else?"

"Not much."

"You saw a group of people arrive by train – we know that. For the last time, before I ask one of my colleagues to stimulate your memory, who did you see?"

"There were uniformed men – military – and men in suits."

"Who did you see in suits?"

"No-one I knew."

I saw the blow to my solar plexus coming and then I felt the pain, and my frantic attempts to breathe, as I lay nearly doubled up. Soon I was alone in the cell, lying on the mattress bed where they had dragged me. I felt sore but guessed there would be no permanent evidence of the interview techniques. I hoped I could get my own back on that man, one day, but it seemed unlikely. My mood swung from defiance to depression, as I thought about my captive state.

I lay there for most of Monday and was only disturbed by the entry of a soldier bringing me a mug of tea and this time a cheese sandwich. In the evening, I was taken out to a car by my two customary guards, who seemed slightly solicitous towards me.

"How're you feeling?" said one of them, a middle-aged man with sandy hair, who seemed suddenly to be human.

"Sore."

"I'm not surprised. Do you want a cigarette?"

"Don't smoke."

"Tell them what they want. If you don't, they'll bring in George, who'll squeeze your balls."

The conversation ended, and I sank into the upholstery, wondering what he meant and where we were going, as they drove out of London, into Surrey. The ride continued along country roads and into a long drive up to a large, detached house with lights on in a few rooms giving a slight glow to a blackened brick exterior. .

I felt my arms gripped tightly, as they went inside, up a carpeted staircase and into a comfortably furnished room, where I saw a man of about sixty, dressed in a dark grey suit that fitted his notion of the costume of the civil service, sitting behind a desk, until he rose and motioned me to a chair on the other side.

"Relax, Mr Butler," he said in a mild, cultivated manner. "We shouldn't be here long. I want you to go home tonight. There are just a few issues to clear up."

Taken aback by his civil tone, I almost said, "Thank you, very much," but stopped in time and said, "I want to know why you are detaining me. If you propose to prosecute me for theft or whatever, why haven't you taken me to a police station and had me properly charged to appear before a court?"

"Not so fast," the other man said, with a smile. "We don't know enough about you yet to consider any such action. That's why you are here."

"But you know where I've been and the humiliating treatment I was subjected to."

"Not really. We can talk about that, later. If you feel you were manhandled excessively, we could think about some compensation, no doubt. But we cannot get that far until I am satisfied with your answers to some important questions about matters that feature in the Official Secrets Act. May I proceed to ask them? By the way, you can call me Peter, and I'll address you by your Christian name also."

I nodded, thinking there was no point in a complete impasse, at this stage.

"First of all, tell me about the person you were with, on your country walk on Saturday."

"I went on my own."

"That won't do as an answer, I'm afraid. You see, Miss Polly Kaufmann remembers you well."

I felt surprise that Polly had told them about me and showed it on my face.

"Not to worry," said Peter, with a smile, "she wants us to let you go. She says you know nothing that might lead to a breach of the Official Secrets Act. Is she right, or is she covering up for you? She told us about your train ride to Cheltenham and back. She says she identified someone on the platform, but didn't tell you. What do you say about that?"

"I'd say she is right. All we wanted to do was to find the whereabouts of a base for use in the event of nuclear war. We found where it is. Now you are threatening us with prosecution, we shall have to keep quiet about it. End of story. Can I go now?"

"Frankly, I find it very difficult to believe you. She told us some other things about the two of you. She said you were close friends, and confided in

233

each other on some problems you have at the college where you work. It seems to me almost certain that she would have said to you, "I think that man on the platform is....so and so."

"Think what you will. I have nothing more to say about it."

"Very well. There is someone I should like you to meet."

Peter pressed a bell and they all waited in silence, but for the ticking of a grandfather clock that suggested to me a boxing referee counting out a man who was down.

Then the door opened and in came Polly, pale-faced and drawn, with a woman in police uniform behind her. To my astonishment, Peter said, "You two have a lot of catching up to do. We'll leave you alone for a while."

With that, he left the room, accompanied by all the guards. I rose and advanced to her, and she clutched his hands, in an agitated manner. "Joe," she said, "I had to tell them."

"Tell them what?"

"That I thought I recognised Ben-Gurion. I told them that I have to support Israel, if I have to choose between its survival and possible downfall. They phoned Ben-Gurion on Saturday and he spoke to me for a long time, and then I had dinner with some Israelis. It was like talking to my mother. They all had relations who perished in the camps. They all came from Germany or Eastern Europe, and knew what it was like to wear a yellow flash on the arm, and to be spat at by other children. They are anti-fascist, like you and me - how could they not be?

And now they have their own country, but no guarantee of security. They want the bomb, just as the Soviet Union has it, as the ultimate deterrent to a potential aggressor. Who am I to say no to them?"

I had a sense of let-down but answered in a measured tone, while awaited what she had to say about their adventure in the base. "I understand your feelings for Israel, which has revived the pride and hopes of many Jews. But the spread of nuclear weapons is quite likely to result in a nuclear war, perhaps not until our children's children are grown up. And what about Israel collusion with the British and French over Suez? Does it make for good relations with the Arabs?"

"No, I told you before, I don't support everything Israel does. They were wrong, and I told Ben-Gurion that. My mother opposed Jewish terrorism ten years ago, even though it may have helped the creation of a Jewish state.

I described my ordeal the previous night, and she kissed my cheek lifelessly. I did not return the gesture, and she had a strained and detached manner, as though she had been scared.

"Were you threatened physically or warned that your life could be in danger?"

"No. But there's something else I have to tell you. The Israeli delegation have invited me to go back home with them. They can get me a job in one of their universities. I have to agree not to say anything about what we saw or heard at the week-end. "

"So that's it. They've bought you off! Polly the rebel!"

She said despairingly, "Joe, I've already made that promise and I'm ready to sign a declaration of secrecy, breach of which could put me in prison in this country – and in Israel. What about you? Will you sign it?"

Before I could reply, the door opened and Peter bounded into the room. "Well, Joe?" he said. "We have a little device that helped me to hear your interesting conversation with Polly. What's your answer to her question?"

Before I had given it a moment's thought, my answer rang out, "I haven't put up with all this captivity and pain for nothing. I'm not giving in."

"Okay, Joe," Peter said calmly, "back into detention you go. I shall see you later."

CHAPTER 19

The detention room, supplied with a sofa, chairs, books and even a vase of flowers, seemed a holiday camp, compared with the underground cell. I knew I couldn't bend or break the metal bars behind the high windows, through which daylight seeped in, and the two guards who came in with the thick sausage and mash that I very much liked were obviously able to deal with any physical encounter with him. One of them, sandy-haired Bert, came in to collect the dishes when I had finished eating, and casually dropped the Manchester Guardian on the floor as he went out of the room.

He came back for it within a minute, but it was time enough for me to see that they had played safe and reported nothing of what I had told them. But they had picked up the Mirror story, and my heart raced as I read it: *"Nurse asks, 'Where's Joe?' Sister Jenny Grainger is looking for her friend Joe, who vanished with another woman near a mystery underground base in the Cotswolds.*

She says she learned that he had gone out to look in the Cotswolds for a secret hideaway intended for government officials in the event of a nuclear war. Jenny thinks he may have been arrested.

She does not believe that Joe has eloped with the other woman."

The reporter said that the Ministry of Defence had told him that they kept stores and surplus equipment on many sites. There was no mystery, though they were not public knowledge, which might encourage attempts at theft. The Ministry spokesman said there was no record of any unauthorised entry and no one had been detained. Anyone who had entered must have got out without detection. He said it was not unknown for a man and a woman to disappear together.

My head spun. I murmured out loud, as though Jenny were in his room, "That's amazing of you - never mind the nonsense about the other woman. It will only make the public more curious about where I am. I wonder if Tony will contact you to say where I am."

Bert gave me a sharp look and then a wink, after he had retrieved the paper. Joe had a moment of hope. Maybe he will relax his guard, so that I can escape. That's fantasy. He'd lose his job and probably get thrown into prison into the bargain. No, that's all nonsense. He's the good cop, pretending to be sympathetic so that I relax my guard and give them what they want.

The afternoon turned into evening, before Peter appeared again, sounding as brisk as ever. "Now Joe, you have some serious thinking to occupy you. There is one condition under which I can let you walk out of here a free man. You must agree to my version of where you have been and what you have been doing. You and Polly were with your friend, Tony – Polly has told me about him - and when he decided he had had enough of the ramble in the

Cotswolds, the two of you decided to make use of the opportunity to get better acquainted. You did gain entry to a Defence Establishment, where you settled down together, but found yourselves locked in. Polly gave herself up to the security guards and a little later on you made a run for it, to avoid possible prosecution for unlawful entry. If you sign a statement to that effect and stick to it, you will hear no more from us. If you refuse, or at any time after your release go back on your word, the consequences will be very severe."

"You mean you'll have me up in the Old Bailey?"

"The stakes are higher than the risk of a prison sentence. Before it got to that, your survival could be endangered."

"I thought Polly had recanted and would soon be safely tucked away in Israel."

"She will indeed. I would forecast she'll settle down there very nicely, and won't cause us a halfpenny of trouble. But if you were to tell stories to the newspapers, she would be questioned day and night by reporters, and if both of you were to tell the same tales, it could be awkward to those of us whose work is to protect the national interest."

"You aren't joking, are you?"

"No, Joe. I'm serious. In the war, I hunted down German spies. There was often a sudden end to their activities, once we had located them. After the war, my job was to help to protect our nuclear weapon secrets, and also to maintain surveillance over communists and fellow travellers who, whether they knew it or not, acted as agents of a foreign Power. Now you are another problem. If you agree to keep your mouth shut and stick to it, you will be free to walk away. Moreover, I think I can say that the trouble you have been involved in at work will fade away. I doubt if the Principal of the College will pursue his charges against you, and we shall forget about the little matter of the fight in the pub."

"So you know everything about me. You make me feel as though I am listening to a caricature of a Marxist lecture about the capitalist state apparatus behind the façade of democratic government, free speech and fair trials."

"All right, if you are being un-co-operative again, we'll leave it for tonight. I shall see you in the morning."

Before I slept, I thought of what Jenny had done. What she was saying in public gave me hope, in place of despondency. It wouldn't do her career any good but she had spoken out on principle. It meant that I would now be supported by a movement of like-minded people.   I knew I would sound paranoid, if not psychotic, to most people, but I was nothing of the sort. The rifle shots fired at me real, not imaginary. I was pursued captured to stop me telling the British people what I saw. I could become a martyr and risk disappearing for good.

But I wasn't dead yet and I knew I could stand up to the hyenas. I relaxed and slept again. The sunburned man came in smiling, and very expertly pulled down my trousers and pants, while the guards held me down. Then he cradled my scrotum in his hand, before pressing it sharply with his fingers, so that a disabling, sickening pain caused me to cry out in agony.

"Okay, sonny boy," the sunburned man said, "it's up to you. Speak when told to and there need be no more trouble for you. Just remember who's in charge here. Now gentlemen, there's no need for you to hold his arms any longer, now I'm on the ball, so to speak."

I felt my arms released, but another sharp squeeze by Sunburn kept me frozen.

"Who did you see in suits?"

"No-one I knew."

The pain became intense as I spoke.

Sitting up with a start, I saw I was on the floor, with the blanket tight round my chest. Daylight was trickling across the washbasin and bucket. Bert was tugging at my arm.

"Come on, young man. What were you shouting about? Get up. We aren't all as bad as you think. Have a cup of tea and pull yourself together. Peter wants to see you. And there's something else. You remember that piece in the paper yesterday about that nurse who knows you – pretty well, I'd say? She took a coachload of women and one man into the Cotswolds yesterday. They got down a quarry and camped out by an MOD storage depot. Big hullabaloo going on. Here's today's paper. Keep what I've said under your hat.

I was fascinated by the reportage:

241

About thirty women and a few men chanting No to Nuclear War and Release Joe and Polly, descended on the Gloucestershire countryside looking for a Regional Seat of Government. They are waving Black Sash nuclear protest banners, and a few Labour Party and Communist Party flags. They have set up a camp outside a cavern down a quarry, where they claim two lecturers at Midland Central College disappeared when they were searching for the RSG.

Tony James, who works at the same college, says he walked with the missing lecturers as far as the quarry and that Butler had since contacted him to say he was being pursued by the police.

Organiser of the protest, Shropshire nurse Jenny Grainger, said, "Bolt holes for government ministers and top officials are preparation for nuclear war. The idea that Britain could wage such a war is sheer fantasy. Civilised life would disappear after the first strike.

"Joe and Polly are on our side and we are on theirs. We want to know where they are."

A statement from the Ministry of Defence said that if the two lecturers committed trespass they must have had personal reasons for entering the storage depot together.

I knew I was no longer on my own. The demonstration outside the bunker was bound to grow and the reporters and cameramen would be there in force. A wave of elation flowed over me but quickly died away. I needed time to think what to do now. Was Bert in sympathy with me or was he playing the part of Good Cop, to win my sympathy and perhaps make me more co-operative with Peter?

My interrogator was as sprightly in his manner as he had been the day before. "All you have to do is to decide whether our statement of your activities on Saturday last is reasonable enough for you to agree to support. That will be sufficient to secure your release. As I have said, after that, there will good practical reasons for you to be well advised to stick to it."

"Can I have a bit more time to think about it?"

Peter puckered his features in annoyance. "I'll give you half an hour. No more."

I was no sooner back in my cell when the door reopened and the sunburned man came in, his face brick-red with fury. "You again! Make up your mind very quickly, or I'll do it for you. My powers of persuasion will make you say anything that I want you to say. Which is it to be?"

As the tough-looking fellow advanced towards me, I hung my head, in passive and defeated mode, designed to put the man off his guard. But my anger rose. I knew I would be beaten up if I resisted, but felt there was no alternative, no matter what happened to me afterwards.

"What are you going to do?" I said slowly, as if in trepidation.

"You, you bastard. But the marks won't show."

The man came forward with his hands by his side, took hold of my ear with a disdainful curl of his lip, and pulled me to his feet. He was so sure of himself, he was unprepared for the heavy punch on his face, as I shouted, "I got the better of you in the

243

flat and now I've given you something else that you'll remember. It's from me and from Edward!"

As my opponent staggered back, with blood on his nose and mouth, I felt a rush of dismay at my own bravado, and braced myself for the attack, knowing I could hardly escape serious hurt when the policeman steadied himself and bore down in earnest.

Instead, the door was flung open and Bert and the third man rushed in and dragged me out and into Peter's room.

"You've done it now," said Bert, who seemed genuinely shocked. "You'll get nine months, easily."

Whether he would be helpful to me again did not matter now. My fate was sealed. I was facing a serious charge of attacking the sunburned policemen.

Peter entered the room and motioned the two policemen to leave.   "He's right, Joe. GBH is a serious offence, and doubly so when it's committed against an officer. What's your excuse?"

"Self-respect. There are limits to what I can put up with."

"I reckoned on that. I thought you would make a gesture of resistance and perhaps mark the officer slightly – enough to enable us to take you to court for aggressive behaviour, if we had to. But this was something more serious.   You'll go down. You've marked the man's face. They'll take photos of it. Don't you care about the prospect of up to a year in prison and the ruin of your career?"

"I'd no idea you were so scheming and manipulative."

"I should think those adjectives would be a fair description of your own behaviour in the last day or two. Never mind the exchange of compliments. If you sign the statement I put to you this morning, I don't think you will have any further trouble. It's in our interest that you settle back into obscurity, and so we shall see to it that the college will take no further action against you over the incidents in the two pubs, and that the local police crackdown on any hoodlums who may feel inclined to damage your car.

"Just use your common sense, Joe. You're just a lonely individual up against a very powerful authority. How about it?"

"Go to hell!"

I saw Peter recoil with the shock of those words, but I didn't feel fury or fright. I thought what might become of me. I was going to be shepherded into a car and back to a cell, somewhere. There I would be left alone for an indefinite period, apart from visits by a silent warder carrying meals. If I was lucky, I would be taken to court and convicted, not of high principle but common assault.

I was taken back to the cell, with slightly more respect than before. I sat down for about an hour, when the door opened and Peter stood there, seemingly as unperturbed as ever.

"Joe, you have some amazing good fortune. It cannot have escaped your notice that we have a new Prime Minister. He is determined to make a new start politically. I won't go into the details but in essence he wants to put the Suez business as far behind him as possible. He would prefer not to have a prosecution and trial and a hullabaloo in the newspapers. He also wants to make light of your trespass on Government property in the Cotswolds. You are the very fortunate beneficiary of a high level decision to downplay your escapades. You can go now, but don't get too cocky. We shall be watching you, and we shall stick to our account of why you entered the storage depot. The press hounds will soon be snapping at your heels. You will be well advised to be very careful what you say. You could still face a charge of grievous bodily harm. We have the photographs."

I looked at my interrogator for half a minute and came to a decision. "I can give no guarantees about what I may say in future. I shall stick it out, go to court if you charge me, and tell the whole story. You will have your account of events, and I shall have mine. I shall call witnesses to testify that I am not aggressive by nature. My case would be that I reacted to the bullying treatment I received from Special Branch. There would be a risk that the mud thrown at me in court would result in the loss of my job and possibly my home. I would describe the underground base, which the newspapers have already publicised, and the Israeli connection, which is bound to go public soon, anyway.

"Suez, the secret base and the smuggling of the nuclear bomb into the Middle East have shredded any faith I had in honest government. It's one big cover-up, as you are perfectly aware."

Peter was now white with barely suppressed anger but spoke calmly. "I would advise you to go before I change my mind. Think over what I have said, and remember that we can always bring you back."

"I know I am vulnerable, but so are you. Public opinion is not a negligible factor and the publicity of a trial could easily build it up into a force that your political masters might have to into account and cause them to question your judgement."

Peter turned on his heel and the two guards took me by limousine with curtains drawn to Euston Station. I walked slowly across the forecourt and bought a ticket back to Birmingham, feeling not quite the failure I had expected to be. It was a shock to see my car parked outside the old house. They thought of everything. They must have broadcast to the regional police forces the registration number of my Morris and recovered the car from near my old school. They obviously found some keys that fitted, as mine were still in my pocket. Inside my apartment, the Matisse ladies hardly stirred as I entered their room. It was business as usual, and after putting the kettle on I turned to the pile of letters on the mat.

The bulky envelope with Jenny's writing on the front made my blood race. It was dated over a week ago and said she had found a scribbled report of my phone call, when she returned from Moscow, with Adrian. She hoped I was well, and wanted to let me know of her impressions of the visit. The rest of her long letter was her travelogue, a fairly standard account of hotels, the ballet, overnight by train to Leningrad, a day in the Hermitage, and the cold weather. I felt resentful that she should have been to Russia and I hadn't. We should have gone together. But I detected no sub-text of meaning, no intimation that she would like to see me or hint of the caring feeling that I still wanted from her, despite the parting. Then I realised that shortly after writing that letter she had put herself at the head of the campaign to secure my release. I told myself, "Don't be petty with pique, she put herself out on a limb, for your sake."

I rang Tony, who seemed startled to get the call. "Are you all right, Joe?" he said, in an uncertain tone, as though not sure of his standing, after deserting his fellow ramblers, seven days previously.

"I'm fine. Don't worry about anything. But if you want to see Polly, you'll have to go to Israel."

"I know, Joe. Amazingly, I had a crackly call from her today, inviting me to visit her. She's just arrived."

"That was quick. Good luck to her. Perhaps you'll end up living over there yourself."

"I wouldn't mind at all. I could have a great time at the seaside. But, what you don't know is that I met Jenny. She came to the college three days ago to ask to see friends of Polly. I talked to her and then we both went to the press and she alerted the Black Sash supporters. She's a great woman."

"I do know that. She rescued my morale from the doldrums when one of my jailers let me see her statement in the Manchester Guardian. I was over the moon when I learned about the demo outside the cavern. That must have turned the tide of my fortunes. I owe you everything, since it was you who spilled the beans about everything, especially where to find the cavern."

"Well, I didn't foresee the consequences when I contracted out of our expedition."

"It's as well you did. Otherwise I would probably have been still locked up."

"And now there's something you should see. Can you pick me up?"

"Sure."

Tony was standing by his garden gate. He put his arm round my shoulder. "I didn't tell them anything they didn't already know. But that's history. I admire what you did. Tell me what you want to, later on, when we have a drink. Drive to the college now, if you don't mind."

Wondering about the slight air of mystery, I did as I was told. As we approached the Victorian building, I was startled to see a very large white cover stretching for yards, above the door. I read the slogans printed in large blue letters, *Hands off Joe Butler! Give us back our lecturer!*

Signed, the Students Union and the Association of Indian Students.

"The Principal's been away and the students have been on picket duty, talking the caretakers out of their natural inclination to take the banner down!"

"What gave rise to this public show?" Waves of surprise, excitement and gratitude swept over me.

"Well, the news story said you were missing, and I told the students you'd probably been picked up by the police when you got into to one of the Government's underground boltholes."

"Thanks, Tony. What you said was right. It will

all come to light. And I guessed it was you who led the women's group to the cavern. "

"It was the least I could do. By the way, no-one believes that you and Polly had a romance. Her sexual leanings are better known than she realises."

"Never mind. She and I don't see eye to eye on all things but I have not lost my respect for her."

I had a foreboding that good fortune could not last, but I found the day went well, except that when I rang Jenny's hospital, I was told she was on leave for a few days. Normal routine came back into play the following morning, after students and staff had finished coming up to me to shake hands. When they asked about Polly, I said she had gone abroad for urgent personal reasons and that I supposed she had told the Principal.

I was disappointed not to see Trevor and wondered if the breach between us had hardened without chance of repair. I found a letter from the union official saying that the Principal had phoned him to say he was he was not pursuing any action against Mr Butler.

After that, Mr Jones summoned me to his presence. He sat hunched in his chair, looking ashen, and I concluded he was suffering from a hangover, after one of his nights out with former shipmates.

"Yes, Joe, the fashionable word for it is dyspepsia, but it's due to the late-night rum, as you probably guessed. What the hell were you up to, last week? Whitehall seems to be all worked up this morning. I told them you were a maverick, always trying to trip me up, but they seemed to want to get you off the hooks on which you have impaled yourself, locally. Why should they bother? Have you got friends walking the corridors of power?"

"I don't think so," I said briskly, not sorry that Jones felt sick. "The powers that be came to the conclusion that I was an upstanding, admirable character, well deserving of the charity for which you are renowned. I assume they convinced you that your mistaken plans to discredit me should be abandoned."

"You're an impudent bugger, Joe, but it's true between these walls that a very senior policeman asked me to lay off you, as the word had gone out from on high that you should be let off the consequences of your foolishness, when you went on some hair-brained project to look for some government warehouse hidden in the countryside. More than that he wouldn't say."

"And this is not the time to tell you. What intrigues me is how these mysterious powers knew about my mishap in the Weavers, and the aggravation I've had from the local idiots."

"And I'm not at liberty to tell you, either, not that I'm very well informed. As I think you know, society is criss-crossed by networks, each one consisting of similar-minded people. One of yours is a network of ban-the bomb supporters, many of them also anti-Israel. One of mine links people who believe that peace is best maintained through the strength of our armed forces. We also uphold the British constitution and the private enterprise economy. You could be a threat to the way of life in this country, one day, but at present you can be allowed to go your own way, subject to our laws."

"Such as the Official Secrets Act?"

"Of course."

"And suppose a parliamentary majority voted to ban the bomb or nationalise the land, what then?"

"We should have to judge how big a threat that was to the British way of life. It might seem possible to reverse those measures at another general election."

I stood up. "Thanks for the lesson in democracy. I must go now. I've a long-standing appointment in Management Studies on the matter of overtime payments."

"Fine. I respectfully suggest you stick to union negotiations, Joe. Your members will appreciate it, and you'll have a happier life. But I don't imagine you'll do as I say."

"I don't suppose I will," I said sharply, with a mounting sense of outrage at Jones' arrogance. All would now depend on the support of my members. Jones was right there. .

I headed towards the refectory, where I was greeted with cheers and banging of cutlery handles on the tables. A group of Indians came up and shook my hand. Teja said, "All's well that ends well, sir. You are a man of independent mind, to quote Robert Burns, and we support your stand against the atom bomb. What about the damn silly accusations about you when we were in the Weavers?"

"It seems it's all over and done with."

"Thank goodness. We've been in touch with our

Embassy. They were going to help us with legal aid if a public slur was cast against us – and you."

"I'm more than grateful to you. I feel we are real friends."

Many more lecturers, some of whom I barely knew, shook my hand, signalling a release of the tension in their manner towards me after the incident in the Weavers. One of them was Ted Groves, the ex-soldier who had supported me on the Suez issue at last year's dance.

Kathleen, smartly dressed and confident-looking, said, "All the best, Joe," as though she had recovered from the disappointment of losing the promotion. I had no doubt that Jones would be inventive enough to find another way to advance her career.

I looked round the refectory for Trevor, but he was not there. After lunch, I decided to call at his home. I still needed the companionship of my oldest College friend, and wondered if it would still be forthcoming.

Margaret came to the door and stared at me. "It's good to see you, Joe. You're quite a star. I heard you were no longer on the missing list. Trev's on a management course this week. Come in and tell me all about it. I'm just putting Hywel to bed." She pointed to a yawning baby, and I made appropriate, appreciative comments, before she took him away.

When she returned, she had combed her hair and taken off her apron. I thought she was comely. It was the only word that came to mind. Her figure, well rounded by motherhood, looked very good.

"You know, Joe, looking back, I quite enjoyed our knockabout comedy here on Boxing Day. I think we are still good friends."

I nodded, and she came over to my armchair, leaned over and gave me a soft kiss on the lips. "You're a local celebrity," you know, "a girl is bound to be impressed."

I shrugged my shoulders but did not return the kiss. She got up smartly and asked me if I would like a drink. "It was only a kiss, boy."

"I know, but I'd better go. I've got a lot of jobs to do to make up for lost time."

"Okay, I'll tell Trev you called in."
.

At home, I reflected on the day's success story, followed by the episode with Margaret that had made me uneasy. "That could have been another impetuous escapade," I told the Matisse ladies. "Do you know what I'm talking about?"

They both seemed to nod, before resuming their air of absorption in the music. That was when the telephone rang.

CHAPTER 20

Mother sounded strained and faint on the phone. "Come round this evening, at about six," she said.

"Are you all right? I was coming round anyway. I've got a lot to tell you."

"I'll see you, then," she said, almost inaudibly, and put the phone down, leaving me with a feeling of guilt for being more concerned about grandma's health, in recent weeks, than hers.

But when I went round, she kissed me warmly on the cheek and said I should get ready to be surprised. I had seen she was wearing her best blue dress, and wondered what she had got up to, to celebrate my homecoming.

She opened the door to the living room. There was Grandma, asleep in bed. She had pulled the counterpane close to her neck, but her strained face looked less pale and withered than it had been when I made my last, dramatic visit to her home.

"We've never been particularly close," Dorothy whispered, "but I can't let her be forced into a home. She wouldn't last a fortnight. So I persuaded her to live with me. She has the downstairs room, where we both have our meals, and I'm converting a bedroom into my own sitting room. We get on all right. The nurse still comes in to see to her."

She added, more dryly, "It'll be convenient for you too, with only one port of call, when you want to see us."

Then she sat down in an armchair by the fire, where the warmth reddened her cheeks and hid the blood that must have rushed there, as she spoke emotionally. She said. "A few days ago, I had a call from your friend, Jenny. I had no idea until then how much she once cared for you and you for her. You gave me no impression that you were very close. I shall have more to say later about this whole situation in which you found yourselves.

"Jenny was worried about you. She thought you might get into serious trouble in your Cotswold adventure. I thought she was right. I didn't know she was going to seek press publicity and organise the women's protest demonstration at the Regional Seat of Government. I understand you don't see much of each other - she says she visited Russia with a boyfriend - and so I invited her round here this evening, to help me find out from you what you've been up to. She has a few more days' leave, and I've told her she can stay the night here, if she wishes."

I froze, and an instant later my heartbeat went frantic, as she rose and skipped nervously over to the kitchen door. She tapped on the panel. Almost immediately, the door opened and Jenny entered the sitting room. I thought how cool and poised she looked, in her light grey skirt and white blouse, looking taller in high-heeled shoes. Her expression was taut but her quick intakes of breath made my blood race, as I sensed her suppressed feeling. Her chest rose and fell rapidly and she smiled as she saw my eyes on them. But she shook hands confidently and spoke breezily, as though she was welcoming a new patient.

"Thanks for all you did for me," I said. "I couldn't wish for a better sister – in more senses than one. It was brave of you to alert the press. It gave you the sort of publicity the NHS may not welcome. I'm sure it helped persuade MI5 to get rid of me as soon as they could."

She spoke coolly, almost casually: "Glad to see you again, Joe. I'm all right. If Eden had still been Prime Minister, you would probably still be imprisoned. MacMillan was just as involved in the Suez fiasco but he has kept quiet about it and has emerged from it unscathed."

"He'll save the Tory Party and restore the American alliance," I said. But I can't repay you for what you have done. Is your job in danger?"

"I doubt it. The Matron was an admirer of the suffragettes when she was a young woman and sees the Black Sash as in a way their successors. However, that's enough about me. What did you get up to in the cavern with a so-called mystery woman?"

"Now you're talking like the *News of the World*," I said sharply. "As you know, the woman was a colleague of mine, as interested in banning the bomb as you are. She had the very good idea of searching for an underground base that was designed to house top people, if the bomb was dropped.

"Right. I do know Polly slightly, and I heard about her plan, which went off at half cock, as she didn't wait to build up support from other members of Black Sash.

"I also know she is not really your type, as I'm sure you discovered.   No doubt you found her an interesting woman, until you learned more about her. I rather fancy that in the process of finding out your male pride was humbled."

"Not at all. She was always just a friend."

She looked at me and shook her head. "I know you better than that. Never mind, just say what happened underground. Having got to the site, why didn't you clear off, and then tell the ban-the bomb movement that's starting up?"

"Are you suggesting that I had some ulterior motive – perhaps with Polly?"

I felt unusually heated at her critical tone, but glad that Polly was not around for questioning.

"I had a lot to explore. Then I was shot at with a rifle, and hunted by the police. I even had to cling like a bat to a high roof to make my escape. If I think about it, my limbs start to ache and my head feels as though it's been coshed. Then I was locked up and threatened with an attack on my life. And I was told I could be sent to prison for assault and battery. Aren't those the important points?"

I grinned at her to offset the sense of melodrama in my story.

"Of course they are," she said, in a more conciliatory tone. "Tell us more."

"Truthfully, I was told that Polly's life, and my own, could be in danger."

The two women looked at me with staring eyes, and followed my every word, as I told my story. A distraction occurred when I saw a movement in a face that resembled a wrinkled russet apple, and then the dark eyes of grandma focused on me. She stirred herself and said, in a high pitched, quavering tone, "Hullo, Joe. This is very cosy. Aren't I lucky?"

"You seem all right, Gran, and you can't get up to much mischief now that mother's got her eye on you."

When I said that, she put her head under the bedclothes, but came out grinning. It pleased me to have attention of the three of them. As I went into details of the scene when the Israeli visitors got off the train in the cavern, Jenny flushed, and cried out, "The Suez link all over again!"

"Yes, it's payment for services given. In return, Israel demands the secrets of the nuclear bomb."

"No wonder they wanted to shut you up. Then a priest helped you to keep on the run. Joe saved by the Church! What a thought!"

"I found a card from Paul when I returned to the college, wishing me well. He doesn't mention anything about our meeting and so I don't think he risks incriminating himself.
He could just be responding to what he read in the press. I shall pay him another visit before long. I don't suppose I could ever convince him that the comfort of religion is illusory, but we have more in common than I would once have thought possible. And I shall see Reuben and Artie. I might even help out in the scrap removal business, if Artie's mate is still on the box."

"Strangers can be very kind," Jenny said brightly. "You also owed a lot to the Chinese girl, who took you in. Was she another friend?"

"She was just a student who gave me some help when I needed it badly."

"You certainly did, especially when they were chasing you, after you came out of the tunnel. You could have been shot dead. It would have been another Crucifixion. That's something you can discuss with Paul. Do you think there would have been a Resurrection?"

"I somehow don't think I would have risen from the tomb. However – who knows? Perhaps my sacrifice might have helped bring on the birth of the ban-the-bomb movement that you mentioned. Something new is needed. Suez has gone quiet for the time being."

"Even though hundreds of Egyptians were killed."

"And even though Eden concealed the truth from Parliament. I wonder how many other Prime Ministers have done that. But I'm not pessimistic. One way or another, it will all come out into the open and I shall then add my story to help expose it. Eden's close colleagues have memoirs to write, and journalists will focus on the Suez fiasco like Jack Russells burrowing into the straw after rats."

"Bear in mind," mother said, "an individual can't make history. It will need millions of people to wake up to the peril of nuclear war, in the near future or in the long term. You've made a good start, but as far as the future is concerned, you must beware of ruining your career or risking your life. I suppose if you were in real danger you could emigrate to Russia."

"I have to say, mother, I don't want to live in

Russia, even if they would have me. I'm British, though not in the Rule Britannia sense. I'll never wave the flag of Empire. What did you think of Russia, Jenny?"

"I thought they'd done some good things. I didn't think much of the special shops for party officials, or old women shovelling snow off the roads. But there's no rich, idle or otherwise, as far as I can judge. I met a little lady with no stylish clothes or airs and graces. She looked as though she might be a shop assistant, but she was the head of all the libraries in Leningrad. I liked that.

"But their invasion of Hungary was a disaster. I can't minimise that, Joe, no matter what you say about keeping NATO at arm's length from their borders. It's stained their reputation as the defenders of democracy in the war and disillusioned probably millions of people all over Europe."

Dorothy went scarlet. She said fiercely, "In this country the class system remains unshaken, but the Russians have done away with it."

Before Jenny could reply, I said, "You are right, mother. At the same time, my point of view on Russia has shifted since I used to come down the stairs as a small boy and listen to the meetings in this room. Then it was utopia. The old political certainties look a bit shaky today. I know now you can't do much to raise living standards in a backward country in a few years, and at the same time mobilise it to meet a fascist invasion - as they did brilliantly. I remember also Stalin being praised to the skies. We know now he was responsible for the execution of innocent people accused of working

261

for the enemy. These were terrible crimes. He was paranoid about security, though the republics really were in mortal danger in the thirties. I have thought about Jenny's point a good deal since she first made it to me. I now think they should have let Hungary go its own way, not only because the desire of the people for independence should be paramount, but also because the costs to their reputation outweigh the gains of a buffer zone to protect their borders."

Jenny said, "Do you think we shall ever follow their path?"

"No, we have a different history. The people will decide the way forward through the ballot box, but we would always have to be aware of the danger of right-wing forces seeking to overthrow the elected government, as happened in Spain."

Mother said vehemently, "I remember General Franco's seizure of power in Spain."

"I know you do, mother, and I have become only too aware of the iron hand inside the velvet glove of state power."

Jenny said, "Capitalism seems to have taken on a new lease of life, after the depressed years before the war. But I'm all for taking nationalisation a lot further than the Attlee government ever dreamed of. The balance of power hasn't changed much, as Joe and I once agreed."

I warmed to her words and could see her pointing to the photograph on the wall of the compartment on the train, on our first meeting. "You are right," I said, "and it isn't likely to happen just round the corner. Democracy has to wrest wealth and power from the privileged classes and the CP understands that. I shall stick to it, rather than join my friend Trevor in the Labour Party. In the meantime, we urgently need a national campaign to get rid of nuclear weapons. Challenging official policies is never easy - there was a great deal of nationalist support for the Suez adventure. Jenny's Black Sash friends are showing the way. That's where I am heading, mother.

"I thought you would stay with the family's politics, but you must do what you feel is right."

"I will, and, by the way, I'm definitely getting an automatic washing machine for you and grandma, as soon as I've taken delivery of the Standard next week. You'll like its pea green colour and its snub nose. All on the never-never, of course. We'll have to see if the new affluence dampens down our socialist feelings."

I saw that the irony was lost on Dorothy, who looked disturbed, and I hastened to reassure her: "Not to worry, mom. I don't say I'm not tempted by status and a well to do lifestyle. A couple of months ago on the train I bumped into a former close friend at university, whose career is going steadily up into the stratosphere. If I made the right noises, it is quite possible he would give me helping hand into a more affluent career."

Her reply surprised me: "It's the risk of hire purchase that concerns me, Joe. We never had credit in our family – we'd rather go without. But these arguments can wait. I'm glad you two have decided where you stand politically, but there are other important things to talk about tonight. Jenny came to see how you were, and you're obviously in good shape. Don't you think so, grandma?"

"I do, but I was just thinking what a fine pair they make." Looking at Jenny, she said, "Are you courting?"

"Not at present. I had a friend, but his views on Russia and socialism in general were so very different from mine, we agreed we had to say goodbye. However, I expect another one will come along, one day."

She spoke very deliberately, as though at a formal interview, for which she had learned her lines. I felt shut out of her thoughts, and sat silent. A long pause was broken by grandma, who said, in a weak but high-pitched and clear voice, "Excuse me, if I am saying the wrong thing, but weren't the two of you fairly close, at one time? There seems something between you, if you'll allow an old woman to express her instincts."

Jenny answered her in a firm, passionless tone: "Yes, we were good friends for a very short time, but a problem arose that could not be overcome, and so we went separate ways. We no longer meet and won't in the future, but we still have the friendly feelings that brought me here this evening."

"I think I have seen a face like yours, a long time ago. Have you ever heard of my son, Edward, Joe's father? He once showed me a photo of a woman with features and eyes similar to yours."

Jenny's composure crumbled. "Joe told me something about his father," she said hesitantly.

Then Dorothy spoke. "I think we are all walking on tiptoe round a delicate matter. If Jenny is the girl

I feel sure she is, Joe mentioned her to me, not long ago. Am I right, Joe?"

I nodded, and she went on in a brisk, no-nonsense manner, "I am afraid I was guilty of keeping a vital family secret to myself, and the result was I hurt the two of you. Only after Joe found it out did I admit to him that Edward had fathered a baby girl born to a political friend with whom he stayed overnight, after speaking at a meeting. Before that, I wondered about Joe's relationship with the girl and knew that what I had revealed to him would put an end to its development. But I allowed myself to believe it was a casual friendship, to avoid having to tell him something that is far more painful to me. I was wrong, and I am very sorry. I only hope it is not too late."

I said sharply, "What are you talking about, mother? I couldn't marry Jenny, even if we wanted that, as she is my half-sister. That's all there is to say, unless there's new scientific evidence that incest is not a bad thing after all."

Grandma butted in again, her voice trembling with the effort. "I don't know, but I think your mother has something else to say. Just give her the chance. It isn't easy for her."

At that, Dorothy started to cry, and Joe put an arm on her shoulder. She looked wretched, as she said, "I am your mother, Joe, but Edward was not your father biologically, though he brought you up with me as well as anyone could have done. Just as Edward was weak one night when away from home, I was weak one night when he was away, and Hairy stayed after a meeting in this house. I never told

Hairy he was your father. I never told Edward. Perhaps I should, but it would have broken up the family and caused great unhappiness all round. But there was no doubt about the facts. So there is no blood tie between you and Jenny. I have no idea where that leaves the two of you. That's all I have to say."

Grandma leaned over and the two older women held each other. I breathed fast, with a hoarse, slightly asthmatic sound. I could not stop myself jumping up and striding into the kitchen, where I leaned against the sink until I felt I could control my feelings of anger and humiliation. I had always seen Edward as my beacon figure. What was he now, or was he no different? He was still the man who had held me in his arms, telling me stories before putting me to bed, and later on helping me with my homework.

With cheeks still flushed, I re-joined the others and said, with studied composure, "I shan't get over this revelation easily. I suppose I should thank you, mother, for telling me the truth, long-delayed as it is. I wish I had known about Hairy. I could have got to know him a lot better. There was always an affinity between us. But I shall always think of Edward as my father. You and he gave me my nurture and love. Most days I think of him and mourn his death. I just wish you had trusted me, all these years, mother."

Dorothy cried again, and Jenny said sharply, "Have some compassion, Joe. I can understand how painful it is for her. It was more difficult for my mother in the sense that she didn't have a husband to help support me, but she welcomed the opportunity to have a child. But because she was married, and because she kept it to herself, your mother must have felt more guilt."

The reproof went home and I toned down my words. "I shan't let it rankle for ever, mother, even though I feel overwhelmed by the thought of all those years of silence on your part. We may even grow closer, now that you've shown a human weakness, instead of being always so certain you were right."

Dorothy's face fell at my candour, but then she managed a half-smile and said, "I had to say what I've always wanted to, but never dared. I am already starting to feel a bit better for it, though I'm very much in the wrong, for not telling you years ago. What do you say, Gran?"

Grandma paused for dramatic effect, looking at each member of her audience, but also building up her energy for speech. She said to Dorothy, "You know that I had a very good relationship with Edward. He was my favourite son. He told me about his one-night affair with Jenny's mother. He said he had confessed to you, but asked me not to mention it to you, or to anyone else. I had some idea about Joe's father, the man you call Hairy. You once told me that he had stayed the night, as if you were starting to say what had happened. You were very upset, and it made me wonder.

"Edward would have told me, if he had known. By the way, I think you were right not to tell him. What you did was all for the best. You accepted his mistake, but he might not have accepted yours. Men expect women to be better than they are themselves.

267

That's life, as we know it. The family – and it was a proper family – was protected.

"However, my own feeling is that enough has been said for the time being. This is Dorothy's house, not mine. She has been very good to take me in. I hope she won't think I'm speaking out of turn if I suggest that we all have a cup of tea and perhaps talk about the weather."

She lay back exhausted by her speech. Dorothy gave her a hug and said, "We can do better than that. We'll have something to eat."

I was not surprised that it was Sunday tea on Monday, with tinned salmon, lettuce and tomatoes, bread and butter, peaches and cream. The question running through my mind was "What now?" I had a bubbling sense of hope, but it was too easy to say that there could be a future for Jenny and me. The two of us had not looked each other in the eyes since Dorothy had spoken. I guessed she felt as embarrassed as I did, and knew the artificial atmosphere could not go on much longer. She was the first to thank Dorothy for the invitation and to say she had better go, before it got too late. She said she had thought of staying, but had a mountain of work to do for her part-time degree studies.

She rose to kiss the other women on the cheek, and then held my pulsating hand for a full half-minute without making eye contact, while saying she hoped I would soon settle down again after the upsets of the last week.

I answered in banal terms of goodbye and good luck, but only felt downcast when I heard her car's engine start. Ten minutes later, I kissed the others good night and drove back home, where I was ill at ease, tense, with no energy in my limbs. I lay on the couch while images of Edward rushed through my mind. I was three and he picked me up from my bed to hold me in his arms, and we listened to the song on the wireless about, *Little man..* Years after that he would discuss Science homework with me and later I was proud to walk out with him in his military uniform. He was still the man I would always think of as father, though I had good memories of Hairy, too. He had always been a friend, whose experiences in Spain had thrilled me. It seemed a pity he never knew he was my biological father, though it was for the best if it protected the family unit, as Grandma believes.

I wondered about Edward's relationship with my mother. It was as though they were happy together but wanted to be free spirits. I thought that perhaps marriage eventually came to seem a bit like a prison. I'll probably never find out.

"You're no good," I said to the Matisse women. "You can't even sing or dance. I shall have to get a television set to take flight from my miserable life. It's time I imbibed the new opium of the people. No Jenny. No Julie, No Jacky. Just me."

I gave Trevor a ring and received a cordial reception. "I miss not having a drink with you, Joe. I've decided I'm not really as ambitious as I thought. The extra money's useful, but it's lonely, even one rung further up the ladder. I don't share the values of the managers. I'm still a shop-floor man at heart. And you were right about the war. It was a sordid affair, and some of us were led up the garden path, though we should have known better. I told Jones that the other day, and he didn't like it."

I smiled to myself, as Trevor got his confession off his chest, in his usual, plain-spoken way. We arranged to go out later in the week. After that I sat back on the sofa and daydreamed about Jenny, vividly recalling our Bournemouth fling. Alf must have had apoplexy when the ceasefire happened.

Then I was standing on the platform before I rushed for the bus back to camp, waving to her and wishing that I had shouted that I would see her on Saturday and that we would go to the pictures in Shrewsbury. The scene switched to my vision of the house that might have been, not new like Trevor's but a hundred years old, with worn stone steps and a push-button that rang a clanging bell at the end of a long corridor. There would have been be plenty of room for a pram, when we had children during the 'sixties, and for meetings with friends who believed that they had to get rid of the atom bomb and change the world. Having convictions was not an optional extra; it was part of living. Edward and Dorothy had known that.

My thought ebbed back to childhood, to the ghosts sitting in the living room, admiring my curls and talking politics. I imagined them filing past me and upbraiding me, in deep voices like Hamlet the elder on stage. Or was there a possibility that Hairy or Lumpy would say, "You did well, boy"?

I became aware that the telephone was ringing, but took some time to reach the phone. A slightly nervous voice said, "I haven't gone home. I thought I should give you a call, so that we could say what we thought in private. It was rather inhibiting at your mother's place, kind as she and your grandma are."

There was silence. At last, I said earnestly, "Your demo at the RSG was amazing. You showed brilliant initiative and publicity flair. You rescued me from giving in to the hyenas or suffering the consequences of defiance.

"I didn't mention something earlier, for fear of worrying mother. I am not out of the wood yet. I shall have to tell people – including the Black Sash - what I saw in the cavern and what happened to me when I was pursued across the fields, and the Israeli link. It's possible that the authorities will be content just to refute what I say, but I could be taken to court, though I doubt it because of the political storm that would blow up."

"But I can understand if you are fed up with me. I let you down a long time ago, as well as more recently. You have an absorbing career, with opportunities to meet glamorous doctors. I must seem like a back number of a magazine that you found in a bottom drawer."

"Stop it! Don't be so negative about yourself. You are a much more principled figure than you allow. I thought you did a wonderful job exploring the nuclear war bolthole. The campaign some of us started on your behalf would be miniscule compared with what would happen if Special Branch went for you again. Forget my sarcastic comments this evening. I felt nervous in the company. I'm still in a daze, now that my half-brother is no more"

"I'm still here, and you are still in my heart. You also embody so much of what I believe in."

"A nice phrase - about my body, though I know you didn't intend it in that sense, but I'm a down-to-earth nurse, remember. The fact is, unless you had an objection, I'd already decided to come to see you right away, to repay the visit that you made to my mother's house. It's your turn to be hospitable. Any problem with that?"

"No problem. What do you say, girls?"

"Who are you talking to?"

"Only my resident ladies, looking down at me from the wall."

"Don't be idiotic. You're like a comedian on stage."

"Funny you should say that. A long time ago, my mother said I liked the limelight."

"Well, you haven't really changed at all, although your enthusiasm for a new car might suggest you are becoming bourgeoisified, in your old age."

"I shan't sell myself that cheap! It would need to be Daimler or a Rolls Royce. But that's unlikely."

"I'm pleased to hear it. Don't forget we had similar homes in some ways when we were growing up. We sort of shared a father and both mothers saw the world through red spectacles."

"And they were right. But the problems we shall face will not be the same as theirs. When I was a kid, the people around me were preoccupied by unemployment, poverty, fascism and a second world war. I hope the situation is different today, though it can't be ruled out entirely that a madman will start a nuclear war. I'm really looking forward to the sixties. Do you think we can face the future together, supporting today's causes?"

"We will, and it goes without saying we'll march

against the nuclear bomb. It's a black cloud over humanity's future. But there is something no-one mentioned tonight. I have never told my mother that I know about her relationship with Edward. I shall speak to her tomorrow about the happy consequences."

"And then perhaps I can start to get to know her by paying her another visit."

"The sooner the better. But tell me, how are the hyenas?

"They have disappeared over the horizon for the time being, at least. Perhaps they have been replaced by a fairy queen.

"I don't know about that. I don't believe in fairies at the bottom of the garden, or anywhere else. I'm a very material woman, and I'm wearing a blouse and a dark skirt, under which is a blue girdle - or have you forgotten it?"

"To quote some words you used earlier this evening, I think you know me better than that."

"I think I do. You're a very nice mixture of romance and politics, and I'm putting the phone down. See you in a short while."

Jenny yearned for me as much as I did for her. I skipped across the room to my pile of records and picked out La Boheme. The aria sung in English sounded crackly and not very strong, but I knew the words by heart, having heard them often enough on my parents' gramophone when I was a boy....*Lovely Maid in the moonlight....*

I smiled at my girls on the wall, and they smiled back at me. Aloofness turned to friendliness, which prompted a response in kind. "You know, she's on her way. Do you think things will go well? She gives me confidence in myself. If I fail this time, I may as well resign myself to a life with you two, but I think we shall stay a foursome. There's no moonlight. It's a cold, rainy night out there, but I see sunshine – more than any artist ever painted."

9 781785 106705